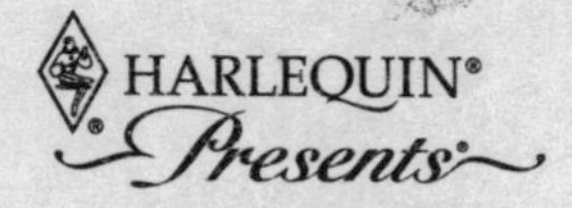

Happy New Year! Have you made any resolutions for 2007?

The editors of Harlequin Presents books have made their resolution: to continue doing their very best to bring you the ultimate in emotional excitement every month during the coming year—stories that totally deliver on compelling characters, dramatic story lines, fabulous foreign settings, intense feelings and sizzling sensuality!

January gets us off to a good start with the best selection of international heroes—two Italian playboys, two gorgeous Greek tycoons, a French count, a debonair Brit, a passionate Spaniard and a handsome Aussie. Yummy!

We also have the crème de la crème of authors from around the world: Michelle Reid, Trish Morey, Sarah Morgan, Melanie Milburne, Sara Craven, Margaret Mayo, Helen Brooks and Annie West, who debuts with her very first novel, *A Mistress for the Taking.*

Join us again next month for more of your favorites, including Penny Jordan, Lucy Monroe and Carole Mortimer—seduction and passion are guaranteed!

She's his in the bedroom,
but he can't buy her love...

Showered with diamonds, draped in exquisite lingerie, whisked around the world in the lap of luxury...

The ultimate fantasy becomes a reality.

Live the dream with more MISTRESS TO A MILLIONAIRE titles by your favorite authors.

Coming in March

The Italian Boss's Secretary Mistress
by Cathy Williams
#2613

Available only in Harlequin Presents®

Annie West

A MISTRESS FOR THE TAKING

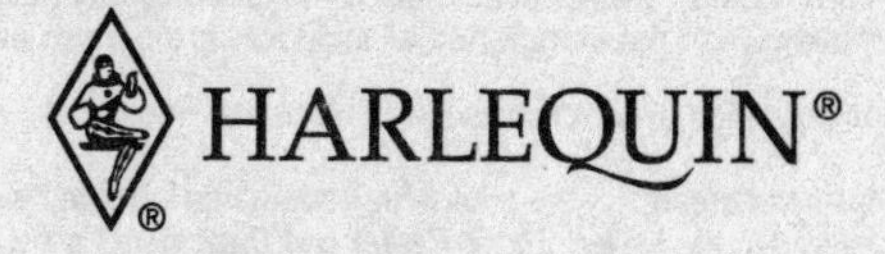

TORONTO • NEW YORK • LONDON
AMSTERDAM • PARIS • SYDNEY • HAMBURG
STOCKHOLM • ATHENS • TOKYO • MILAN • MADRID
PRAGUE • WARSAW • BUDAPEST • AUCKLAND

ISBN-13: 978-0-373-12600-2
ISBN-10: 0-373-12600-X

A MISTRESS FOR THE TAKING

First North American Publication 2007.

This edition published by arrangement with Harlequin Books S.A.

www.eHarlequin.com

Printed in U.S.A.

All about the author...
Annie West

ANNIE WEST spent her formative years on the east coast of Australia. She got hooked on romance early. In her teens she spent long afternoons playing tennis with her best friend, and in order to recover between games, they'd stagger to her friend's house, where there was an unending store of Harlequin books.

Fortunately she found her own real-life romantic hero while studying at university and married him. Despite the distraction, she completed her honors degree in classics. She decided against a postgraduate degree and took a job in the public service. For years Annie wrote and amended, redrafted and revised government plans, letters and parliament reports. All good grounding for a would-be author, especially since, in Annie's case at least, the first draft is rarely final.

Annie decided to write romance when she took time off to raise her children. Between preschool and school activities she produced her first novel. She also discovered Romance Writers of Australia. She's active in RWA's writers' groups and competitions, attends annual conferences and loves the support she gets from so many other writers. She had short stories and a romance book published in Australia, but it wasn't until late 2005 that she found the success she sought with Harlequin.

Annie lives with her hero (still the same one after all this time) and her children at Lake Macquarie, north of Sydney. You can contact Annie at www.annie-west.com.

To Claire, Andrew and Geoff—for your inexhaustible patience and support.

To Joanie for the encouragement. To the VGs for believing (and rereading). And to the superlative Karen—where would I be without you?

Thank you all.

CHAPTER ONE

RONAN CARLISLE scanned the glamorous crowd filling the hotel reception room. A snake like Wakefield couldn't have this many friends.

Yet there were always people wanting to get close to the rich and powerful. Ronan had no time for sycophants himself, but then he didn't have Wakefield's need for fawning admiration.

He glanced past the Sydney Harbour view to where Wakefield preened amongst his cronies. The sight made him want to plant his fist in the man's smarmy face. But that would only bring temporary satisfaction.

Soon, very soon now, Wakefield would get his just desserts. Ronan would make sure of it.

He felt a swell of savage anticipation. Tonight he'd let slip a hint as to his next major commercial move. No doubt by morning Wakefield would be eager to follow suit. And that was when Ronan would bring him down. It was simple. It was ruthless. And it was long overdue.

Ronan shrugged his shoulders free of their stiffening tension and turned to leave. But something in the colourful, noisy room caught his attention. *Someone.*

Over the artistically coiffed heads he saw her move away from the entrance to plunge into the crowd. She was alone, starkly dressed among the throng of decorative trophy wives and well-fed executives. A woman with a purpose, he decided, as she carved a path through the party. It was there in her glittering dark eyes, in the jut of her chin, in her palpable aura of determination.

She paused to ask a question, then changed direction. Towards Wakefield.

In that moment Ronan decided he'd stay a little longer.

Instinct told him the party was about to get a whole lot more interesting.

Marina took a deep breath and forged on. Triumph warred with fear as she neared her goal, and her heart thumped a telltale double beat. Her palms were damp, but she resisted the impulse to wipe them down her skirt, just as she ignored her trembling knees and the nervous roiling in her stomach.

You can do this, Marina. You have to do it.

It's your last chance.

She almost wished she'd grabbed a glass of Dutch courage from the waiter. But she needed all her wits, not to mention luck, for this confrontation. Failure was a luxury she couldn't afford. Not when her whole future and her family's depended on it.

So she pushed her way through the crowd, as out of place as a household tabby cat among a coven of pampered Persian thoroughbreds. She felt curious eyes on her and lifted her chin a notch. She had important business with Charles Wakefield and nothing, not his evasion tactics nor her own trepidation, would stop her this time. Previously, his minders had stonewalled, pretending he was too busy to see her. But tonight he'd have no choice!

She was almost at the windows when her skin prickled.

She raised her eyes and stumbled to a halt, ensnared by an intense indigo gaze that seemed to blaze straight past her protective barriers and delve into her inner fears. Her throat dried as she stared up into the face of the man who stood head and shoulders above the crowd.

A stranger. She'd never seen him before. And she knew from the press cuttings that he wasn't Wakefield. But his unblinking scrutiny held her motionless, confused.

The party hubbub faded, replaced by the heavy beat of her pulse, loud in her ears. And still she couldn't look away from that compelling stare.

His was a stark face, hard and intriguing. Beyond handsome. His height and the breadth of his shoulders signalled pure masculinity. But, more than that, she was mesmerised by the barely leashed tension in him, as if he were poised for action.

Potent. Vital. Commanding. The words tumbled through her brain as she swallowed hard and fought against the swirl of heat, heavy and low, that rippled through her.

Then there was a shout of laughter, someone jostled her, and a movement ahead revealed her quarry.

Wakefield stood by the windows, smiling confidently. He looked exactly what he was: one of Australia's wealthiest men, scion of a famous business dynasty.

This was her chance. She had to concentrate on her mission, on Wakefield. Yet she didn't move. She stared at him, but it was the presence of the dark-haired man looming nearby that filled her mind. She felt his eyes on her still, and her skin heated with sizzling awareness.

She resisted the temptation to turn her head and meet his look again. She couldn't let herself be sidetracked. Not now.

Taking a deep breath, she marched over to Wakefield, the man who'd ripped her world apart.

He was shorter than she'd imagined, barely her height. But he had a smile like a crocodile. A shudder of apprehension slithered down her spine at the sight of it.

'Mr Wakefield.'

Her voice was too strident, loud enough to make all eyes fix on her. Heat flared in her cheeks as conversation around them stalled. At the same time the stranger moved forward into her line of sight. A group of women gathered close, welcoming him.

Annoyed that she'd even noticed, Marina dragged her attention back to Wakefield.

His eyes flicked over her, cataloguing the plain suit, flat shoes and neat hair. His brows rose, and she stiffened at the dismissal she read in his face. She'd had a lifetime to get used to the fact that looks weren't everything, and she'd be damned if she'd let him judge her like that.

'I'm Marina Lucchesi, Mr Wakefield.' She plastered on a

smile and held out her hand. If her face felt stiff and the smile forced, it was the best she could do.

Recognition flared in his eyes. Then it was gone, lost in the give-nothing-away blandness of polite enquiry.

'Ms…Lucchesi.' His grin made her long to snatch her hand away. 'Welcome to my little celebration.' His handshake was brief. 'Do you work for me?'

Before she could answer he continued. 'If it's a message from the office, sweetheart, you'd better talk to my assistant.' He half turned. 'Damien! Take the message.'

'No, Mr Wakefield, I'm not an employee.' Her voice betrayed her anger, but she didn't care. He knew exactly who she was. 'But I am here on business. I was hoping to arrange a private meeting with you.'

'Ah. Damien.' He turned to the sleek young man who'd appeared beside him. 'Ms Lucchero wants an appointment. Organise something for her. Perhaps with recruitment.'

'It's *Lucchesi,* Mr Wakefield. Marina Lucchesi.' She stepped forward, deliberately crowding his personal space, and felt a jab of satisfaction as she got his full attention. 'I'm sure you remember the name. After all, you know my brother, Sebastian.'

Know him well enough to strip him of everything he owns. And a few things he doesn't own as well.

She didn't say it out loud, but the knowledge pulsed between them, raw and undeniable. His eyes widened and Marina waited, poised for his inevitable acknowledgement.

But it didn't come.

'I'm sorry, Ms…*Lucchesi,* but I don't recall. I meet so many people.' He spread his hands and looked around his entourage. 'Very few of them make an impact on me.'

Marina ignored the stifled titters and kept her gaze fixed on her nemesis. A wash of embarrassment scalded her cheeks and throat. It was the final straw.

Fury such as she'd never experienced surged through her, stiffening every sinew in her body. She'd expected stonewalling, murmurs of regret or, if she were lucky, a reluctant agreement to meet and discuss the situation. Naïve as she was, she'd actually believed she'd be able to reason with the man. Bargain for more time.

She hadn't expected scorn. Not from someone who had nothing to gain from humiliating her.

'You surprise me, Mr Wakefield.' Her voice was harsh and unsteady, but no way would she back down now. He might have her brother's measure, but he was about to find out she was a completely different proposition.

She pitched her voice to carry. 'Surely you should remember the name of the man whose company you stole.'

The whispering voices ceased abruptly and a tense hush fell. Marina felt her heartbeat thrum heavily once, twice, three times, before she continued.

'Or is that such a common occurrence you don't recall those details either?' She stared straight into his wrathful eyes.

The frozen silence lengthened as Wakefield's companions leaned closer. A decisive movement to Marina's left caught her attention and she looked up.

And up. Into the deepest, most amazing eyes she'd ever seen. Ink-blue and fringed with long black lashes, those same eyes had held her in thrall only minutes before. Now they sizzled with a dangerous heat.

Up close, the man was stunning. It wasn't just the aura of power he wore like a mantle, or the innate authority of a height well over six feet. It was the combination of strongly angled cheekbones, sharply defined jaw, authoritarian nose and slashing dark eyebrows. No wonder the women clustered so close around him.

Abruptly the stranger moved. He broke eye contact, inserting himself between her and the avid onlookers, murmuring something that made them reluctantly step away. He made the manoeuvre seem deceptively easy.

A minder of Wakefield's, she decided, still dazed by the inexplicable fizz of reaction that bubbled through her veins. She'd never felt anything like it before. And then to discover he worked for her enemy, was a yes-man to Charles Wakefield… The moment shattered in ridiculous disappointment.

Wakefield found his voice again, his smooth tone laced with

a venom that demanded all her attention. She turned back to face the ire of the man she'd just accused.

'I'm afraid, Ms Lucchesi, you're completely in error.' His eyes iced over and she shivered. 'You shouldn't make such accusations when you don't know the facts.' He lowered his voice. 'That's slander, sweetheart. And it can be a costly mistake.'

A cold, hard knot of fear plummeted through her stomach and she sucked in a gasping breath. What more did this man want? Blood? Hadn't he taken enough?

Dimly she realised that the tall bodyguard and Wakefield's assistant had moved the onlookers aside. Nearby people laughed and gossiped. But here, in this small circle of quiet, she stood alone. Face to face with the man who'd destroyed her brother's future and her own.

'I see you're having second thoughts about your accusation.' Those wintry eyes regarded her steadily, and she read satisfaction in the slight curve of his mouth.

It was the look of a man who knew he'd won.

What the hell! He couldn't take anything else from her. There was nothing left to steal.

'No,' she responded. 'No second thoughts. You and I both know it's true. What else would you call duping an innocent out of his inheritance?'

To Marina's surprise, Wakefield cast a frowning glance at the imposing man beside them. Did he have qualms about airing his dirty linen in front of his staff? Surely his underlings were used to cleaning up the mess left behind by his dubious business practices?

'Ms Lucchesi.' Wakefield spread his hands and offered the semblance of a smile. If it weren't for his eyes, as cold as a reptile's, she might have been taken in by it. 'There's obviously been a misunderstanding,' he continued. 'Your brother hasn't told you everything.'

'So you admit to knowing Sebastian?'

He shrugged. 'I remember him now. A very...impetuous young man. But hardly an innocent.'

Not by the time you got your claws into him, she thought.

'And you call it legitimate business practice to steal a prosperous company the way you did?'

She saw his sidelong look at the man to his right.

'Come, come, Ms Lucchesi. Marina. It was hardly theft.'

He was denying it, damn him. Brazening it out. Marina clenched her fists at her sides so no one would see how they shook. She'd never hit anyone in her life. But now, face to face with this slick playboy, she was so close.

'You say it's normal commercial practice,' she asked in a voice no longer her own, 'to get a twenty-one-year-old so drunk he doesn't know what he's doing? Then get him to sign your legal documents?'

For a single shocked moment no one spoke or moved. Even the two men flanking Wakefield seemed to stiffen. Then he spoke, as smoothly and patiently as if reasoning with a child. 'Your brother obviously knew you'd be upset and didn't give you the full picture.'

'That's a lie! I know exactly what happened and—'

A deep voice interrupted before she could get into her stride. 'Surely this isn't the time or the place, Charles? Why not take this somewhere more discreet?' It was the bodyguard who spoke and, despite her anger, Marina couldn't ignore the responsive shimmer of deep-seated excitement as his words seemed to roll across her skin.

Wakefield scowled. 'And give this lunatic accusation any more credibility? Thanks for the suggestion, but I can take care of my own business.'

'Like you've taken care of Ms Lucchesi's?' came the dry response.

Marina stared at the man who dared to interrupt the tycoon. One of his dark eyebrows rose in a slashing line of enquiry as he stared down at his boss. His square jaw was tensed but his tone had been mild. He didn't seem at all fazed by the fact that he'd just taken issue with his furious employer.

Whoever the guy was, he didn't scare easily. Charles Wakefield had looked at her with dislike. But it was nothing compared to the naked hatred in his eyes as he glared at the man beside them.

'I'll thank you to keep out of this, Carlisle. The woman's misguided, but I can handle it.' He looked over Marina's shoulder, not even sparing her a glance. 'Ah, here's the chief of security now.'

'No need for that,' said the man, Carlisle. 'I'll escort Ms Lucchesi.'

Like hell he would! She still had plenty more to say to Charles Wonderboy Wakefield.

'No way! I'm not finished yet.' Incensed, she glared up at the man beside her. 'If you think you can keep me quiet about what he's done you're dead wrong.'

Slowly he shook his head, and she thought she saw understanding in his eyes. Maybe he didn't always like doing his job, but that wouldn't stop him performing his duty. That much was obvious from his determined face and the implacable set of his broad shoulders.

'It's not a matter of keeping you quiet,' he said, dropping his voice and moving close so that the heat of his body radiated against hers. 'You can't win this now. Not here, like this.'

There was a bustle of movement and Marina tore her gaze away to take in the group of thickset men in dark suits that closed in to circle them. Charles Wakefield was already talking in an undertone to their leader.

'Official security,' said the man beside her, nodding at the newcomers, who seemed all brawn and muscle. 'You've got a choice now. You can let them frogmarch you out of here as an intruder. They'll probably hold you till the police come to investigate Wakefield's complaint that you're trespassing or disturbing the peace.'

He paused, his gaze holding hers.

'Or you can leave with me.'

As if she could trust him. He was Wakefield's man. And, more than that, her sixth sense warned her not to take him at face value. He was up to something.

Outraged, Marina spun round, but another dark suit blocked her view. Piggy little eyes stared back blankly at her from a face that gave nothing away.

Carlisle was right. Wakefield would have her tossed out. It wouldn't do to upset his guests with anything as unflattering as the details of her story.

'I can promise to get you out of here with your dignity intact.' Carlisle's low voice whispered in her ear and she felt the seductive temptation of his words.

Escape. Solitude. Safety. They beckoned strongly.

But she had to resist their lure. This would be her only chance to confront Wakefield and she had to try again, no matter what the consequences.

She shook her head, then felt a large hand close on her elbow. Carlisle's touch was light but insistent as he bent again to feather words against her ear.

'It's not running away,' he urged, as if he could read her mind. 'It's regrouping. You need to find a better approach.' He paused, and his warm breath on her skin sent a little tremor of pure female awareness down her spine.

'Unless you'd rather be arrested,' he concluded, with a finality that made her jerk her gaze up to his. But there was no threat in his expression, only the truth.

Just then a hand took hold of her other elbow, its touch more than firm. Hard fingers bit into her flesh and she winced as she swung round to face the newcomer who'd been getting his orders from Wakefield. There was no sympathy in his face. No expression at all.

Her luck had just run out.

She'd promised Seb she'd take care of everything, as she always did when he got into strife. But instead she'd let her emotions override her common sense. She'd just blown her chance to fix this nightmare.

Outrage warred with guilt and despair as she realised how irrevocably and disastrously she'd failed.

And suddenly, shatteringly, the physical weakness she'd been battling all evening was back. It crashed over her in a debilitating wave. Her strength drained in an instant, so it took all her energy to remain standing.

The doctor had warned her not to overdo it. To give her

injuries a chance to heal. Now it seemed he'd been right. The tremor in her legs told her they'd give out soon. And she couldn't face the humiliation of pitching to the floor at Wakefield's feet.

Defeated, she slumped. Immediately a strong arm wrapped round her, dislodging the grip of the new security guard. Carlisle obviously had some authority.

He held her close to the solid comfort of his body. 'No need to bother seeing us out,' he said blandly over her head. 'I'll make sure Ms Lucchesi gets safely home.'

Wakefield's face twisted in annoyance. He opened his mouth as if to protest, then shut it, watching the man beside her with wary eyes.

'Goodnight, Charles. Gentlemen.' Carlisle nodded affably to the group. 'It's been an unexpectedly…interesting evening. We'll see ourselves out.'

And then they were strolling across the room. At least she hoped that was how it looked. Only the two of them knew it was just the superb strength of his arm, clamping her to his side, that prevented her collapsing.

Determined, she focussed on the far side of the huge room, intent on forcing her protesting legs to match his easy pace. Her breathing was shallow, as if she'd run a mile, and now the pain was back, tearing at her greedily.

'Can you make it to the door?' His voice was a whisper of air against her scalp. And once again it was enough to set off a chain reaction as tiny explosions of sensual awareness detonated through her body.

At any other time she'd worry herself sick at such an instinctive response to any man, let alone a stranger. But right now she was too busy fretting about whether she'd collapse before or after Charles Wakefield called in the police to arrest her on some trumped-up charge.

'Yes, I'll make it.' She gritted her teeth.

She felt all eyes on them. The discreet whispering doubled as they passed. But this time the attention wasn't because she stood out from the crowd with her chainstore suit and Amazonian figure. As the heads swung their way, she assumed it was because of her accusations. Then, as the throng pressed close and she saw the rampant speculation on so many female faces, she realised the crowd's interest centred on the man beside her.

Several people spoke to him, faces eager. And each time she heard the deep tones of his reply. But he didn't stop till his way was blocked by a man, vaguely familiar, with an air of authority. Her companion introduced her, so she stretched her lips in a smile and held out her hand. But their short conversation was a blur, muted by the throb of pain passing through her aching body. Then they were on their way again, step by slow step towards the exit.

Through the doors and into the foyer, where the relative silence was like a comforting blanket. Almost as welcome as finding it deserted. No bodyguards. No police. Relief was a buzzing hum in her ears.

She stumbled to a halt and took a long, slow breath, combating her physical pain and the sudden renewal of that dreadful roiling in her stomach. Reaction, that was what it was, after that horrible scene.

'Here.' Carlisle's voice was peremptory as he ushered her to a low divan tucked against the wall.

'Thanks. I'm fine now.' She tried to disengage herself from his hold.

'You don't look it,' he responded, watching her carefully. 'You look like you're about to fall down.'

She gave up trying to push his arm away and stared back at him. 'Well, I'm a lot tougher than I look,' she said, with a spark of her old self.

Deep blue eyes stared straight back, and she had the unnerving sensation he could see everything she tried so hard to hide. She swallowed convulsively and looked away.

'Please let me go.' To her surprise his arm dropped away immediately, making her shiver again, this time at the loss of his body heat. 'Thanks for your help. I appreciate it. But I can look after myself from here.'

Still he didn't leave, but stood watching her, head tilted slightly, as if considering her words.

And then there was no time for dissembling. With more haste than grace she collapsed abruptly onto the cushioned sofa as her knees gave way.

'Don't move,' he ordered, as he spun on his foot and strode back into the reception room.

As if she could.

She grimaced, wondering how on earth she was going to get out of here under her own steam. She let her head fall back on the upholstery and felt her exhausted muscles relax.

'Here, drink this.' A hand, enveloping and warm, took hers and curled it round a cold glass.

'Thanks, but I can manage *that* all by myself.' There was nothing wrong with her hands, just her legs. She took the glass and sipped iced water, ignoring his harsh expression as he hunkered beside her.

Immediately she regretted her spurt of temper. It wasn't his fault she'd wrecked her chance to make Wakefield see reason. Or that she was as weak as a kitten. And he *had* stuck up for her back there with his boss.

'I'm sorry,' she said. 'You've been great, really.' She sighed, 'It's just—'

'Don't worry about it,' he cut in, his tone impatient.

His gaze held hers, and she wondered what a man like him was doing working as hired muscle for Charles Wakefield. His take-charge attitude and the intelligence she read in those stunning eyes seemed to fit him for so much more.

'You'll be all right if I leave you?' He cut across her thoughts as he stood up to loom over her, making her even more aware of her own physical weakness.

'Of course. I'll just catch my breath.'

He nodded brusquely and turned away, pulling a mobile phone from his pocket as he headed across the lobby.

Idiotically, she was disappointed he'd taken her so readily at her word. She'd insisted on being left alone, but now she felt bereft.

Rather than watch him return to his post, she shut her eyes, trying to work out how she'd get home. She'd come by bus, several of them. Did she have enough cash for the luxury of a cab? If not, she was in trouble. She didn't have the strength to walk four blocks to the bus stop.

She sighed and leaned back against the cushions, weary beyond belief. Now her head was thumping too. Tension, she decided. And the way she'd scraped her hair back from her face didn't help. She reached up, pulling out the pins that kept up her unruly hair. No matter now if she looked like a wild woman. She'd blown her chances with Wakefield—the one she'd wanted to impress.

She groaned at the memory of that disaster, and knew she had to get away. Now. She slid closer to the edge of the sofa, ignoring the way her skirt rode up in her haste.

Psyching herself for the effort to stand, Marina opened her eyes. And caught her breath at the sight of the man standing in front of her.

It was him, Carlisle, frozen as if in mid-stride on his return. For the first time she saw him whole, not as a shoulder to lean against or a pair of probing eyes. And what she saw made her stare, transfixed.

He had *it.* Sex appeal, animal magnetism—whatever you wanted to call it. Something more vital and compelling than mere good looks. And infinitely more dangerous. Especially when he looked at her like that.

Heat prickled as her skin seemed to contract across her. The sensation made her intimately aware of all those completely feminine places that responded immediately to the promise of such a man.

And right now his look *was* a promise. All masculine intent and blazing energy that made the air between them crackle with electricity.

Her shallow breath stalled in her throat even as her heartbeat accelerated into overdrive.

Then, as suddenly as if it had never been, his expression changed, morphing into hard, unreadable lines. She blinked. Was she seeing things, or had that scorching look been real?

He returned her gaze steadily, hiding nothing, and she felt the guilty heat creep up her neck, as if he'd been able to read her crazy thoughts.

Yeah, sure. As if a man like him would look at her that way. Marina Lucchesi, the least glamorous woman she knew. Too tall, too buxom, too outspoken Marina. She dropped her gaze to the empty glass cradled in her hands.

'Marina.' Reluctantly she looked up. He stood over her, brows together and legs planted apart. Again she felt the flood of physical awareness that made her tremble. 'It's time to go. I'll take you home.'

'And why would you want to do that?' she asked, still breathless.

His lips tilted up in a smile that disturbed rather than reassured. 'Because I'm the man who can get you what you want—Charles Wakefield's head on a platter.'

CHAPTER TWO

A KNIGHT in shining armour, come to slay the dragon and rescue the damsel in distress?

Yeah, right.

Marina stared back at him, wondering whether she'd developed a hearing problem. Or maybe it had been a double vodka and not mineral water in the glass he'd given her.

One thing was for sure—no man, other than her father, had ever offered to solve her problems. And she was old enough to know it was never going to happen again.

'I don't believe you,' she said flatly. 'No one's got that much power.'

Something shifted in his expression. Nothing she could put her finger on. But the effect was clear—creating a look of pure arrogance. One that would have done Charles Wakefield justice. It was enough to make her shiver again.

'You think not?' he murmured eventually. 'Perhaps you're right. Decapitation might be too drastic. Maybe we could settle for him getting his just desserts.' And still there wasn't so much as a flicker of humour on his face.

'And pigs might fly,' Marina muttered.

She ignored his outstretched arm and reached over to place the empty glass on a low table. Then she planted both hands on the edge of the sofa and levered herself up.

Immediately he put a hand to her elbow, steadying her. But it wasn't enough, not with the way her knees shook. In one decisive movement he scooped her off her feet and gathered her close.

It happened so fast, shock held her speechless for several seconds. His eyes locked with hers. Dimly she registered the hard heat of his body against hers, the seductive aura of safety, the temptation just to let go.

'What do you think you're doing?' she breathed, all too aware of the reception in the next room. 'Put me down!'

'Why? So you can fall at my feet? I'm not that desperate for female adulation, thanks.'

All the fear and hate and anger she'd felt towards Charles Wakefield coalesced instantly and unreasonably into a blaze of fury directed at this new tormentor. Her palm tingled with the barely repressed impulse to smack him on the cheek.

'I said, put me down. Now!'

He didn't move a muscle, simply stood, watching her, as if her weight was no strain at all. While she felt as helpless as a newborn. And ridiculously conspicuous. Any second now someone would come out and see her, slung like a sack of potatoes in his arms. It would be one more humiliating detail in the saga of her defeat.

'I'll yell,' she threatened.

This close, there was no missing the spark of interest in his eyes. 'I thought you wanted to leave with a minimum of fuss,' he countered. 'Or was I wrong? Do you get some sort of turn-on from being the centre of attention?'

She gritted her teeth at the injustice of that remark, fearing if she responded she'd do something stupid like shout.

Meanwhile he looked her over slowly, cataloguing her reaction to his question. Her hands clenched into tight fists, her chin lifted and her chest rose and fell rapidly in her agitation. His gaze paused as she took a deep breath, and instantly heat blossomed and spread through her. She tried to slow her breathing, calm the riot of confused emotions that had tipped her out of control.

Her eyes dropped, following the direction of his, and she saw that her jacket had come undone, revealing her plain white shirt and, through the fine material, the equally plain white bra that covered her ample breasts.

She opened her mouth to say something, anything, but he turned his attention back to her face and the babble of outrage died in her throat.

His eyes looked *hot.* There was no other way to describe them. They seemed to sear her with their intensity, and she blinked, trying to read his expression. But he gave nothing away. Nothing but that odd, compelling flare that made her want to wriggle out of his grasp.

Or curl in closer to his solid strength.

No one had ever held her like this, and she was aware of a myriad of disturbing new sensations. His arms curved round her body and stockinged legs, generating an intimate warmth that both teased and comforted. Her head rested against his shoulder, cheek pressed to the hard plane that sloped down to his massive chest. His own scent, clean and masculine, teased her senses. No heavy manufactured aftershave for this man. Why bother when you had the real thing?

'Well, what's it to be?' he asked, in a deep, soft voice that stirred a swirl of response low inside her. 'Do we go quietly or do you make a scene?'

'Of course I don't want a scene.' She glared at him, furious that he had the upper hand. Furious that she'd just discovered another fatal weakness to add to her list: chocolate, black and white romance movies, speaking her mind, and deep blue eyes that sizzled with promise.

Damn it. She didn't need this now. She just wanted to go home, where she could lick her wounds and regroup.

As if he'd read her mind, he swung round and strode across to the lift. Automatically she reached out and pressed the button.

'Shouldn't you be getting back to the reception?' she asked, trying for a tone of polite interest. As if being cradled in the arms of the sexiest man she'd ever met was no big deal.

'No, I was ready to leave,' he said, watching the numbers above the lift light up as it ascended.

'But don't you need to get back to your work? To Charles Wakefield?'

He looked at her then, one dark eyebrow raised. 'Work for Wakefield? Just who do you think I am?'

The bell pinged above her head and the steel doors slid open with a refined hiss. The mirrored walls of the lift reflected images of the pair of them as he carried her in.

Those images were enough to banish any last shred of Marina's self-confidence. She hung like a broken doll in his arms—skirt hiked up, long legs dangling, jacket askew and, worst of all, her wild tangle of dark hair frothing in all directions.

'You can put me down now,' she urged as the doors slid to, shutting them into the confined space.

'Push the button, would you?' He ignored her request, and when she didn't move to help hefted her closer, so that her face was half buried in the silk of his shirt while he hit the button for the ground floor.

His heart beat strongly somewhere beneath her face, and the scent of him intensified, musky and compelling. Despite her better judgement she breathed deeply, and felt stupidly disappointed when he relaxed his hold a little so she lay back against his arm again.

'Honestly, you can let me go now. I'm perfectly capable of standing.'

'You still haven't answered me.' His eyes locked with hers. 'Who is it you think I am?'

She shrugged with the shoulder that wasn't tucked in against him. 'Aren't you some sort of minder? The way you moved those people away so they couldn't hear…'

Her words petered out as he laughed. It started as a grin, then grew to a rumble in his chest and eventually to a deep, infectious sound that almost made her smile.

'You think I'm one of Charlie's lapdogs?' For the first time since they'd met his expression was uncomplicated and unguarded. Sheer amusement lit his features and dazzled her. He had the sort of smile that was guaranteed to melt the most level-headed woman in ten seconds flat.

'I wouldn't say lapdog,' she answered, remembering the way he'd put Wakefield on the spot. 'But you sure had his interests in mind. The way you manoeuvred that crowd away was obviously to protect him.'

His smile faded. 'It didn't occur to you that perhaps *you* might have been safer accusing him somewhere private? Didn't you stop to think how he'd react if you confronted him in front of his adoring fans?'

Anger resurfaced at his accusations. Especially since she knew he was right. She should have kept her cool, not lashed out at Wakefield's provocation.

'If I spoke the truth, you mean?'

'Exactly.' His tone held no apology. 'When you deal with a man like Wakefield you need to understand there's a time and a place for open honesty.'

'It sounds like his dubious morality has rubbed off on you,' she accused. 'Is that how you operate? By choosing to be dishonest? I don't know how you stomach working with the man.'

His hooded eyes met her gaze as he let the silence grow between them. And, though he didn't react visibly, something about the increasingly tense atmosphere in the enclosed space made her uneasy, convinced she could sense a barely leashed anger thrumming through his big body.

The doors slid open, but still he didn't respond to her jibe.

Marina didn't know whether to be relieved or dismayed as he stepped out and, without pause, carried her straight across the glossy mosaic floor of the huge foyer. They were in Sydney's most expensive hotel. And as they made their way past a smiling concierge and a couple of curious guests she wished she could simply disappear.

'If you plan on fighting Wakefield, Marina, you'd do well to remember that things aren't always what they seem.' His words were low, for her ears only.

Then they were outside. She felt the warm air brush across her hot cheeks as they left the air-conditioning, and she concentrated on avoiding eye contact with yet another uniformed employee. She needn't have bothered—all his attention was focused on Carlisle.

'Your car's right here, sir.'

'Thanks...Paul.' He read the young man's discreet name tag.

'Here you are, sir, madam.' The employee stepped out under the enormous *porte cochère* and opened the passenger door of a car.

It was a long car, silver and streamlined. Marina didn't know much about the latest models. But you'd have to live on the moon not to realise that this fine beauty had cost more than several times the average annual wage, and was probably one of a kind in Australia.

For some reason the sight of it scared her almost as much as the confrontation with Wakefield.

'I *said* you can put me down, and I mean it,' she whispered fiercely. 'I'm not going anywhere with you. I don't know who you are. And even if I did, I'm okay now. I can make my own way home.'

His answering smile probably looked intimate to any onlooker, but this close Marina could see the anger in Carlisle's eyes. It radiated from him in waves, so sudden and so unmistakable that her own eyes widened.

'By all means don't trust me,' he said as his gaze pinned hers. 'That's probably the most sensible thing you've done all evening.'

And now once more his expression was unreadable, but something there, something unsettling, sent a tickle of apprehension down her spine. She knew without being told that this was a man she didn't want to mess with.

'But,' he continued, 'don't for one minute expect me to let you wander off at this time of night, alone and barely capable of standing, let alone driving.'

'I wasn't going to drive,' she burst out. 'I'm not that stupid.'

'My car can get you home just as safely as any taxi,' he said implacably.

No way was she going to tell him she'd planned to use the buses. It was absolutely none of his business. But at the moment she didn't have the strength to fight it out. She felt as forceful as a rag doll.

'Mr Carlisle? Is everything all right?' asked the youth waiting at the car door.

'*Mr* Carlisle?' Marina repeated. She'd assumed that was his first name.

'That's right,' he said as he strode over to the sports car and carefully lowered her into the embrace of butter-soft moulded leather. 'Ronan Carlisle.'

His smile flashed, devastating despite the dimness of the car's interior. He took her right hand in his. 'A pleasure to meet you, Ms Lucchesi.'

Marina's hand was limp in the hard warmth of his. The brief pressure of his fingers curling around hers sent a tide of sensation tingling across every nerve-ending. But she barely noticed. She was too busy absorbing the truth of his identity.

If the sheer power of his personality and his arrogance in the face of her protests hadn't been sufficient to convince her, this car would have been proof enough. Or the look of hero-worship from the guy who'd opened it for them. And then there'd been the cluster of women crowding around them as they left the reception. She remembered the avid excitement on their faces, the hungry looks.

Marina sagged back into the luxurious leather and tried to make sense of it all.

'Don't faint on me now, Marina.' His voice was a low purr near her ear as he leaned across to snick her seatbelt shut.

'I'm not about to faint!' How dared the man? He must have an ego as big as Charles Wakefield's. 'I'm just tired.' She lifted her chin a fraction and glared into the knowing eyes mere inches from hers. 'And I never said you could take me home.'

His silent laugh was a puff of fresh, warm breath across her cheeks. More intimate than the embrace of his arms about her. She felt again that insidious, melting sensation begin deep inside her.

'Come on, Marina,' he urged, voice grave despite the twinkle of amusement in his eyes. 'Let me take you home. I'd worry all night if I left you to make your own way.'

Staring back at his handsome, determined face, Marina wondered why she'd even bothered to argue. Suddenly exhausted, she gave in to the force of the inevitable.

'Thank you. I'd appreciate it.'

And that was how, still reeling from the debacle with Charles Wakefield, Marina found herself chauffeur-driven home by the most disturbing man she'd ever met.

Ronan Carlisle.

Who also happened to be one of the richest, most powerful businessmen in the country.

CHAPTER THREE

RONAN let the silence lengthen as he buckled his seatbelt and started the car.

He didn't need to look at his passenger to know she'd used her last reserves of strength. Despite her fighting spirit, Marina Lucchesi had almost reached breaking point. The shadows of fatigue under her expressive dark eyes, the uncontrollable tremor that racked her body. The exhaustion etched in the pallor of her face. They all told their story as eloquently as any words could have done.

She wasn't up to dealing with a piranha like Wakefield.

Hell! She was so physically weak she shouldn't be out of bed. The woman had more spirit than sense. And how she'd managed to get past security in the first place to confront Charlie-boy was a mystery.

Easing the car into the street, he stopped at a set of traffic lights and flicked a curious glance at her.

She stared straight ahead, either not seeing or not acknowledging his look. Her shoulders slumped and she bit down hard on her full bottom lip. His gaze lingered a moment on her mouth before he turned his attention back to the street.

Who was she? A virago with a grudge against an ex-lover? Wakefield was a womaniser who played the field. Or was she what she claimed, the sister of an innocent victim of his dirty business tactics? Ronan's gaze narrowed. And why was she in camouflage, wearing that shapeless suit? He'd felt the seductive curves beneath that prim navy outfit and there was no doubt in his mind Marina Lucchesi would be worth much closer investigation.

He'd lay odds no one had spoken to Charles Wakefield like that in a very long time. If ever. Ronan silently applauded her nerve. If the confrontation hadn't been so dangerous for her he would have laughed outright at the look of shock on Wakefield's face.

She'd managed to stun Wakefield into rare silence. And even on the verge of collapse she'd used her sharp mind, and tongue, to keep Ronan at a distance as well, when he'd tried to help her.

She had guts.

And that mouth. She used it like a weapon.

He'd like to see her use it for other things. Those luscious ripe lips, with their natural pout, had to be the most erotic he'd ever seen.

His lower body tightened as his mind lingered on the possibilities.

The lights changed and he slid the car forward. Over the noise of the engine revving he caught another sound. A groan or a sob?

'What is it?' he demanded, shooting her another look.

'Only the usual,' she answered, with obvious sarcasm. 'Wondering how I came to have public arguments with two multimillionaires in one night. It must be some sort of record.'

He smiled. Down, but not out. Marina Lucchesi was some woman.

She sighed. 'Not my usual Friday night.'

'And what *is* your usual Friday night?' He was genuinely interested. She was the most intriguing woman he'd met in a long time.

'Not business launches with the jet-set.'

'Hardly the jet-set,' he countered. 'There were a lot of hard-working people there.'

'And a lot of glamorous ones who'd never worked a day in their lives.'

He let that slide. There'd been the usual hangers-on. The sort who loved a free party.

'You should have told me,' she said after a minute's silence.

'Told you what?'

'Who you are,' she said flatly. 'I feel a complete idiot.'

'I don't see why.' He worked hard at keeping his face, if not his name, out of the press. Unlike Wakefield, he shunned the media hype, enjoying his relative anonymity. He didn't look for or want instant recognition.

But her silence was accusing, not understanding.

'Maybe you're right,' he admitted. 'I could have told you earlier. But it didn't occur to me at first—I was too busy wondering if you were going to slip into a dead faint.'

'And later?' she persisted.

Good question. Why hadn't he told her? Because he'd got such a kick out of their verbal duel? Because he'd been too intrigued by his immediate reaction to her to bring the interlude to a close? The combination of her no-holds-barred attitude and obvious fragility had aroused his protective instinct. And his hormones.

'It was refreshing talking to someone who didn't watch every word they said. Who wasn't worried about making an impression.'

That was an occupational hazard these days.

'You shouldn't beat yourself up about tonight,' he continued, knowing how mentally bruised she must be after the confrontation. 'Why do you think Wakefield was so worried? He couldn't keep you quiet. He knew you had the mettle to make trouble for him.'

She shifted in her seat. 'But it didn't help, did it? He's got away with it and there's nothing I can do. Absolutely nothing.'

Did he imagine a quiver in her voice? He swung the car over to the kerb.

'Why are you stopping?' she asked, turning swiftly as if to get her bearings. Her long hair flared round her and he caught her elusive scent again—warm and fresh as spring sunshine.

'I'm waiting for directions,' he answered. 'I don't know where you live.'

'Oh.' Her lips formed a perfect inviting circle, and it was an effort to force his gaze up to her eyes.

'Head north,' she said. 'Either the bridge or tunnel will be fine. But if you're going in the other direction you could drop me at a taxi rank.'

'I'm on the north shore myself.' He watched her steadily. 'Tell me where you live, then sit back and shut your eyes. You look dead tired.'

She frowned, and he knew it wasn't what she'd wanted to hear. What woman would?

True to form, she straightened her shoulders. Then she pushed her hair back behind her ears, twisted it round and up high in a style that seemed too heavy for her slender neck.

'Damn,' she whispered.

'What is it?'

'No pins,' she mumbled, and let the long tresses fall in a rippling curtain that hid her profile and the over-bright glitter of her eyes.

He felt a surge of protectiveness and almost reached out to touch her. But he guessed it was only pride that held her together right now. She wouldn't thank him for his sympathy.

And he knew instinctively it wasn't only sympathy he wanted to give.

'Give me your address,' he repeated. 'I'll take you home.'

She didn't know what woke her, but suspected it wasn't the car stopping. She sensed they'd been stationary for some time when she opened her eyes and found them parked in her driveway. Then she realised that the movement-activated sensor light at the corner of the house was off, confirming they'd been sitting there for a few minutes at least.

There was no light in the car, and very little from the street at the end of the drive. She could barely make out the man beside her in the gloom. Yet she knew instantly that he was watching her. The intensity of his scrutiny raised goosebumps of awareness across her flesh, bringing it to tingling life.

'You should have woken me,' she said, her voice grating with accusation. For there was something unsettling about his very stillness. And the sensation that he'd been focussed on her so totally, watching her as she slept.

Despite the sultry summer air she shivered, conscious of an unfamiliar expectancy in her shortened breathing and rapid heartbeat.

'We've only just arrived,' he countered, his voice giving nothing away. 'And I didn't think another minute or two's rest would hurt.' He opened his door and she blinked at the blaze from the interior lights.

Then he was out of the car and opening the passenger door, while she fumbled to get her seatbelt undone. She looked up to see him lit by the exterior house lights that had switched on as he moved.

Big, broad across the shoulders and powerful, he loomed over the car. Even his exclusive tailored clothes couldn't conceal the aura of dominance that he projected, his sheer potency. His sleek silk shirt, stylish jacket and dark trousers should have branded him as one of the socialite A-list crowd they'd left behind at the reception. But instead they revealed him for what he was: a man used to command, utterly formidable.

And, to any woman, a danger. Attractive was too bland a descriptor for him. With those strong, sharply defined features he was compelling. And the passion that seemed to lurk in the indentations at the side of his mouth was enough to warn her that she was way out of her league.

Just looking up at him made her heart race.

'Marina?' His brows drew together, then in a single fluid movement he bent to lift her out of the car and tuck her close against his chest.

The heat of his body, the faint male aroma, the strength of his arms were familiar now. Almost welcoming.

She must be out of her mind.

Last time he'd carried her she'd been in shock—almost able to pretend she didn't react to his blatant maleness. But now she couldn't think of anything else. He filled her senses, deluging her awed brain into overload with a new awareness. The firm texture of his jaw when she accidentally brushed it. The way her body fitted so perfectly in his arms. The odd incendiary flare of excitement in the pit of her stomach.

'I can stand, thanks.' But her voice sounded breathless instead of sure. She cursed this stupid feminine response to sheer masculine appeal.

Typically he ignored her, and strode instead to the patio and up the steps towards the door just as easily as if he carried a child. Not a woman a mere couple of inches under six feet.

Hastily she dug out her key and slipped it into the lock. 'Thanks very much.' She looked up at his face, deliberately not meeting those eyes that seemed to see far too much. 'I'm really grateful for the lift. So much better than waiting for a cab,' she babbled.

'My pleasure,' he responded, in a low voice that brushed, like the sensuous silk of his shirt, right across her nerves. But instead of lowering her to her feet, he nudged the door open and stepped inside. Automatically Marina reached out and hit the light switch by the door, illuminating the wide hallway.

'Which way?' he asked as he followed the hall.

'I'm fine now that I'm home,' she countered, wriggling in his arms, as if she could make him release her. 'I can stand by myself.'

'Marina.' He stopped and looked down at her, eyes unfathomable, but with an infinitesimal smile that deepened those tiny grooves beside his mouth. 'You've got nothing to worry about, I promise you. Tonight, all I want is to see you safely tucked up for the night.'

Of course that was all. A man like him would never be interested in someone like her. Even if he were a playboy like Wakefield, who apparently couldn't resist the lure of the chase, she'd have nothing to fear. She wasn't beautiful, or glamorous, or sexy. She didn't even have experience on her side.

He simply felt sorry for her because she'd made a fool of herself in front of Sydney's business elite. And because she couldn't get her damned legs to work properly. That was all.

She didn't want his pity.

Her eyes burned with the glaze of unshed tears. Tears of anger at her failure tonight. At her inability to make Wakefield atone for what he'd done. At the sheer physical exhaustion that had hit again so suddenly. And at the knowledge that this man, this unsettling stranger, had seen her at her most vulnerable.

She tilted her chin and pointed down the hall. 'The third door on the left is mine,' she said, refusing to look at him. His intentions might be charitable, but, selfish as she was in her pain and frustration, she wasn't in the mood right now for anyone's charity.

He paused at the open door and once again she reached round to flick on the switch. Soft lights illuminated the familiar room, with its soothing blues and creams. She almost sighed aloud at the sight of the bed, with its coverlet turned down ready for her.

Every bone in her body ached with tiredness, and she couldn't even summon the energy to be annoyed any more that Ronan Carlisle had ignored her protests and invited himself into her home.

And then he was lowering her onto the bed, as gently as if she was some fragile piece of glass.

She sank back gratefully against the pillows propped at the headboard.

'I'm sorry I snapped at you,' she offered as his gaze took a swift inventory of the room. She saw the way his eyes lingered on the crutches in the corner and the medication on her bedside table. Then he turned to look at her and she hurried on.

'It was churlish of me. And I do appreciate your help. I don't think I could have made it back here by myself.'

He ignored her thanks and asked brusquely, 'There's no one else home? No one to help you?'

Marina bit her lip against the sudden shaft of pain his words evoked. She was tired. She was having trouble holding her emotions in check.

'I live alone,' she said. 'And I'm quite able to take care of myself.'

His frown told her he wasn't convinced, so she added, 'My brother lives ten minutes' drive away,' and gestured to the phone on her beside table. 'If I need anything I can always call him.'

Male that he was, Ronan Carlisle would be satisfied with the idea of a man to look after her. He wouldn't have any idea that it had always been she who'd looked after Seb.

For long moments he stared down at her, and then he nodded. 'Okay. Do you need any medication?'

She glanced at the box of pills. Surely not tonight. She'd been trying to do without them because they left her feeling so woolly-headed. And after what she'd been through she was so exhausted she'd sleep as soon as her head touched the pillow. But you could never be sure.

'If you could get me a glass of water that would be great. The kitchen's down the hall and the glasses—'

'I'll find them,' he said as he turned on his heel.

As soon as he was gone she felt better, not tense with the need to appear self-sufficient. The tightness in her chest eased and she carefully swung her legs over the side of the bed. The *en suite* bathroom was only a few feet away, and the unsteadiness in her legs had abated. It must have been brought on by the stress of confronting Wakefield.

She'd washed her face and finished brushing her teeth when she heard him in her room.

'The water's on the bedside table,' he said in a low voice from just the other side of the door. 'Do you need any help in there?'

'No, I'm okay now.' Wimp that she was, it was easier to stay there in the bathroom than open the door and face those penetrating eyes.

'Thanks very much for your help,' she said, in what she hoped was a bright voice. 'If you wouldn't mind pulling the front door closed firmly behind you, it's self-locking.'

Silence for a moment, then he said, 'I'll remember.'

'Thanks again…' What should she call him? Mr Carlisle was too formal after all that had happened, but she couldn't use his first name. 'Goodnight, then,' she murmured eventually. But there was no response.

She stood by the basin listening, but there was nothing. He'd already left.

See? He just felt sorry for you. He knew you were safe now at home and he couldn't get out of here fast enough.

When she opened the door the bedroom was deserted and dark. Only the bedside lamp spilled its warm glow. He must have been trying to save her a trip across the room to switch off the overhead lights.

Ronan Carlisle was thoughtful, all right, as well as stubborn and self-opinionated and way too good-looking. Marina yawned again and reached under the pillows for her nightie.

She undressed and slipped the cool midnight-blue silk over her head. It cascaded in lovely concealing folds down her body and she smiled at the thought of this one private indulgence. You didn't have to be a size eight beauty queen to enjoy the feel of sexy lingerie against your skin.

She put her folded clothes on the blanket box at the foot of her bed and straightened to reach for the crutches. She'd better find the energy to go and check the front door or she wouldn't be able to sleep.

'Here, let me.' That familiar dark voice came from the doorway and she swung round, stunned, to meet Ronan Carlisle's shuttered gaze. Her pulse beat a crazy tattoo that might have been shock—or excitement.

In one hand he held a large steaming mug, and as she watched he strode across the room and snagged her crutches in his other. He put the mug on her bedside table and reached for her, his big hand hard and hot against the tender bare skin at her elbow.

A shimmer of exquisite excitement emanated from his touch.

'Where do you want to go?' He held the crutches out to her, but she couldn't tear her gaze from his face. It was there again, the blaze of heat in his deep blue eyes that liquefied her bones.

And then, seemingly in an instant, it was gone. His faced showed only polite enquiry. Mild concern. No more.

'Marina?'

'I thought you'd left. I was going to check the front door,' she said, wishing she had a robe at hand to cover herself. Though, she reasoned, the nightgown covered a whole lot more than some of the dresses she'd seen tonight.

Still, she couldn't shake the awareness that she was almost naked in her silk and lace. And he was so close his body heat radiated against her. It seemed to stoke a fire down low in her abdomen. She felt the flames curl and flare as his indigo gaze meshed with hers.

'Come on, you shouldn't be on your feet.' He sounded gruff, and his expression was stern. As if he feared he'd have to scrape her up off the floor when her legs gave way.

But it wasn't her injuries that turned her knees to jelly. Not this time. It was something else. Something new.

Desire.

An unfamiliar tension gripped her body and slowed her brain as he guided her to the bed. Automatically she leaned against his arm as he supported her to sit down.

Without a word he swept the sheet further aside, then bent to swing her legs up. His hands closed round her heels, lifting them onto the bed. She sucked in a breath at the tingling shivers that spread in ripples up her legs.

Immediately he stilled.

He must feel it too—her uncontrollable trembling. Fervently she hoped he'd put it down to her weakened physical condition and not realise it was reaction to his touch.

She stared at the dark head so close to her own, at the way his ebony hair flopped down over his brow. The fan of his dark lashes against his skin. What was he thinking?

Her heart thudded against her ribs as she waited, willing him to let her go.

That was what she wanted. Wasn't it?

He moved infinitesimally and the tremors grew. His long fingers slid from her heels to her ankles, encompassing them in the lightest of caresses.

Marina bit down hard on her bottom lip to stop the sigh of pleasure welling in her throat. The slide of his hands against her skin felt so unbelievably good. Warm and gentle and…erotic.

Her fingers curled, twisting into the sheet beside her. She held herself rigid as his hands skimmed higher, inching up her calves.

And all the while the swirling heat in the pit of her stomach intensified. The tremors became shudders as he reached her knees and discovered the sensitive flesh behind them.

She couldn't contain her automatic jolt of response to his touch. It was as if shards of white light splintered through her, numbing her brain and momentarily blinding her.

What was happening?

This had to stop. Now!

'Please…' To Marina's horror her voice was a hoarse plea, revealing exactly how little control she had over her body.

'Please, I—' Abruptly the words were lost as he raised his head.

Was this the same man? His face seemed pared down to the arrogant bone, his mouth a taut line, nostrils flared wide. And his eyes… She shrank back against the pillows. Those eyes were voracious, glittering in a way that unnerved her.

'Since you ask so nicely, Marina.'

She heard his low murmur through a haze of disbelief as he

settled beside her, hip to hip, on the bed. His body heat burned her through their clothes.

Her throat closed on her instinctive protest, so she raised her hands to ward him off.

She was stunned, but she wasn't stupid. She didn't want him to—

He leaned forward and her hands pressed into the silk of his shirt, felt the solid muscle beneath and the rapid thump of his heart.

She tried to concentrate on pushing him away. But somehow her fingers slid instead across the sleek fabric, moulding the hard, living heat of him. A heady surge of scorching sensation coursed through her fingertips, her palm, right through her body, fusing all thought.

Transfixed by a wanton tide of longing, Marina felt his hands settle on her bare shoulders. The slight roughness of his skin against hers, masculine against feminine, made her shiver.

Dangerous. Far too dangerous.

She had to protest, find the words that would stop this madness.

But he leaned close and her vocabulary disintegrated.

He lowered his head to hers and she forgot to breathe.

CHAPTER FOUR

RONAN'S lips were hot, hard and demanding. At their touch, Marina gave up all effort of resistance.

Suddenly she knew with absolute certainty: this was exactly what she wanted.

His tongue thrust into her open mouth and dark heat consumed her, blotting out everything but him. He pressed her back into the pillows, his body conquering hers, his arms pinning her against him.

There was no hesitation in his kiss. No doubt. Just a driving urgency that should have frightened her. She felt consumed by his power, his remorseless, compelling energy.

But Marina wasn't afraid. She exulted in the hard strength of his body against hers. In the insistent thrust of his tongue caressing her and the hot, musky, drugging taste of him in her mouth. The erotic flavour of him was surely addictive. Like the spicy scent of his skin that filled her nostrils and short-circuited her brain.

She was on sensory overload, absorbing and responding to layer upon layer of new experience. There was nothing about this man she didn't want. Didn't *need.*

She loved the sensation of his torso pressing her down against the bed, the weight of him both comforting and tantalising.

Desire, like hot honey, flowed through her, loosening her muscles, making her pliant in his arms.

His hands splayed across her cheeks, fingers speared into her hair, holding her so he could deepen the kiss, delve further into her mouth. She welcomed him, eagerly answering his demands with her own.

She gave him back kiss for kiss as the fire inside her grew into a molten flow deep in her belly and right down to the junction of her thighs. She arched into him, revelling in the amazing sensation of his chest crushing her breasts.

Yet she wanted more.

His hand slid across her shoulder and she shuddered as every nerve-ending exploded at his touch. It was like fire, delicious flame, stroking down her body. She trembled as his hand closed on the silk at her side, exploring the curve of her waist. She couldn't prevent the sinuous twist of her lower body in response.

And lower went his palm, circling over her hip and dipping down.

Sanity crashed upon her like a breaker on soft sand.

His hand slid across her thigh. She stiffened, rigid under his touch, as the magic shattered. From the sensual fog of desire reason slowly emerged. Then caution. And fear.

Instead of clawing into his shirt her hands pressed, frantic to lever some distance between them.

For an instant he didn't budge. But his hand stilled.

Then with one final, heartbreakingly seductive caress of his tongue against hers, he released her mouth and pulled back.

Marina sobbed in a gulp of air, distraught at the mix of relief and longing that swamped her. She could still taste him on her lips.

She told herself she was relieved he'd stopped. She'd done the right thing in pushing him away.

She just wished she'd never let it start.

Her body was on fire from their shared passion. But it was embarrassment that flamed in her cheeks.

She couldn't meet his eyes.

'I don't want—' But his finger on her lips stopped her.

'Of course you don't.' His deep voice cut across her whirling thoughts with the precision of a stiletto.

Startled, she raised her eyes, but he'd already got to his feet, was turning away. All she saw of his face was the taut angle of his jaw and the furrow of his down turned brow. And then he was walking away across the room.

Marina let her hand slide to the crumpled sheet beside her, still warm from his body.

She wasn't regretting her last-minute qualms. Of course she wasn't. Nor was she upset at how readily he'd agreed to end their kiss.

Their sensuous, mind-blowing, once-in-a-lifetime kiss.

She drew another slow, calming breath.

He turned in the doorway to face her, but in the dim lamp-light his face was shadowed. She couldn't read his expression, could only see the enigmatic gleam of his eyes.

Even that was enough to send another spiral of fierce need twisting through her. What had this man done to her? How had he breached a lifetime's defences so easily?

And how had she been reckless enough to let him do it?

'Goodnight, Marina,' he said, in a voice blank of all emotion. 'I'll make sure the front door is locked on my way out.'

Marina slumped back against the pillows, her heart pounding.

She strained her ears, listening to the faint echo of Ronan Carlisle's footsteps on the polished wood floor. The sound of the front door closing behind him.

Silence.

Except for the roaring of blood in her ears.

She lifted unsteady hands to her cheeks. Her face burned. Her chest heaved as if she'd been running for her life and her nipples were sensitive peaks. Even the delicate touch of her silk night-gown created an exquisite tension there.

She could taste him on her tongue. Feel his powerful hands on her face, in her hair. And deeper, lower, where the sensation of need still agitated, she registered the searing liquid heat of desire.

So this was lust.

She covered her swollen lips with her fingers, stifling the rising bubble of hysterical laughter.

Marina Lucchesi in lust!

It had taken her long enough. After spending a lifetime attending to her family, her home and honest hard work, she'd finally discovered temptation in the form of an attractive man.

And what a man!

If the situation weren't so awful she'd have to laugh. Either that or cry.

How could she have given in to the rush of insane desire that welled at his touch? She'd been pathetic.

Nothing had prepared her for this torrent of emotion, this longing.

Her only hope was that he'd attribute her reaction to the strain she'd been under, to her physical weakness.

And, of course, to his own stunning attractiveness. He probably had women melting at his feet all the time. He'd have the pick of them. Wouldn't have to settle for second best.

She guessed he'd only kissed her out of curiosity.

Or worse: pity.

She squeezed her eyes shut against the scalding tears of embarrassment that filmed them.

Stupid. Stupid. Stupid.

At least he'd had the decency to stop when she had changed her mind. He'd pulled back when she'd stiffened in his arms. If he'd kept up his sensual onslaught, she knew the interlude would have ended very differently.

She hiccoughed on a laugh. Or was it a sob?

Even her strict upbringing and her own inclination not to be noticed by the opposite sex hadn't saved her. She'd made an utter fool of herself.

If only she'd used her brain rather than simply let herself drown in sensation. If only she hadn't willingly colluded with his sensual demands.

Her pride wouldn't be so bruised if she'd repulsed him because she never slept with strangers.

But she didn't even have that salve to her pride.

It hadn't been morality or caution that had made her pull back. It had been the realisation that at any moment his big callused hand might slide up under her nightgown to discover the disfiguring network of scar tissue that deformed her thigh.

Maimed, and anything but beautiful. That was her.

Even if pity had motivated Ronan Carlisle to kiss her, he couldn't feel *that* sorry for her. The sight of her injured leg would make any man recoil. Especially a man used to the sultry charms of glamorous women.

At least there was an upside, she realised with a bitter twist to her lips. Her injuries would undoubtedly have repulsed Ronan, so she'd escaped the final humiliation.

She'd never have to reveal to a man of his experience and expectations that, at twenty-four, she was still a virgin.

The next day dawned hot and bright, but it was late by the time Marina showered and breakfasted. A night of broken sleep and the unsettling memory of Ronan Carlisle guaranteed she was slower even than usual. Desperately, she thrust the image of him from her mind.

She was impatient for the day she'd be fully healed. The physiotherapist said she was almost there, but to Marina it sounded like hollow reassurance, designed to keep her trying.

She shouldn't complain. Others weren't so lucky. Blinking away a tear, she busied herself, packing her towel and purse into a tote bag ready for her aqua therapy.

The phone rang as she headed out the door.

It would be Seb. She didn't want to break the news that Wakefield wouldn't give them more time. Or admit that she'd blown it and got the man so incensed he'd called Security to throw her out. The memory of Wakefield's cold, uncaring eyes made her shiver.

With a sigh she dropped her bag and trudged into the kitchen. Might as well get it over and done with. Delay wouldn't make the task easier.

She reached for the phone, but stopped dead as the answering machine clicked on and the deep voice that had echoed through her confused dreams filled the room.

'Marina, it's Ronan Carlisle. We need to talk. I know how you can get your company back.'

He paused for a long moment and her stomach muscles

spasmed tight. She swayed and reached over to lean on a straight-backed chair. Dismayed, she registered the sense of deep foreboding that held her rigid.

And, worse still, a flare of unwelcome excitement.

Then his voice continued smoothly. 'Call me. I have a proposition for you.'

CHAPTER FIVE

RONAN leaned back in his chair and watched the restaurant entrance.

He was early, deliberately so, staking his claim on the territory. It was second nature to take the advantage when beginning an important negotiation.

He smiled, savouring the thought of it.

Marina Lucchesi. She'd be obstinate, he had no doubt. And critical, accepting nothing at face value. She had a quick mind and enough guts to make her a formidable negotiator, even though he was the one in the position of power. He held all the cards.

A flicker of heat flared in his belly. He recognised it instantly. Anticipation. It had been there last night, and again this morning, when he'd woken to the dawn light and lain in the semi-darkness thinking about Marina.

She'd been so passionate, so responsive, that he was eager for more. Eager for the intimacy his frustrated body had craved through the long hours of darkness.

It had taken every shred of his resolve to pull back from her as she lay in his arms. Even now the tension in his lower body was almost painful at the memory of her generous sensuality. But he hadn't mistaken her change of mind. That sudden recoil from his touch had been obvious. It had been the wrong time. He shouldn't have let things go so far and so fast.

He'd bide his time. Marina would be worth the wait.

There'd been reluctance in her voice earlier today when he proposed this lunch meeting. Perhaps she was embarrassed at how completely she'd responded to him. Women had some strange ideas, he knew.

Or was there another reason? He propped his elbows on the table and tapped his fingers together. Despite all he'd learned about her, Marina Lucchesi was an enigma.

She was confident, capable, supremely passionate. But there was an unusual reserve about her.

When they'd kissed, for an instant she'd been startled, uncooperative. She'd seemed…unsure, even clumsy, as if untutored.

He shook his head at the absurd notion. After a few moments she'd kissed him back with a fervour that had sent his temperature soaring and his blood pressure rocketing off the scale. She was one seriously sexy woman.

So why had she seemed uncertain at first?

Innocence? He discarded that possibility. There was too much innate sensuality in Marina for it to have remained untapped until now.

Was she playing some sort of game? Trying to pretend to a hesitancy she didn't feel? What could she hope to gain by that? He sat back, sure he'd find out soon.

He knew she had misgivings about meeting him, but she was desperate too. And desperation would win out over caution. He counted on it.

Marina wanted her family company back, for herself and her brother. And to protect their employees. His digging had unearthed some interesting facts. Including her absolute loyalty to the firm's workers. No way would she leave them to Wakefield's tender mercies without a fight.

And then there was her other weakness. He savoured the memory of last night's promising interlude. She might be wary, but she couldn't hide the way she reacted to him. He could use that knowledge to ensure she didn't walk away.

A movement outside caught his eye, and he sat up straighter as he saw her approach from an avenue of trees in the park opposite. No crutches today. She walked slowly but steadily. He was relieved she hadn't done any permanent damage after the way she'd almost collapsed at the party.

She'd pulled her hair back again, this time in a long plait, and she wore…what was it? Some sort of loose tunic dress, a couple of sizes too big for her and styled for a middle-aged matron.

He frowned, wondering what message that outfit was supposed to convey. Hands off?

He grinned. *Too late for that, Marina.*

Then she stepped out from under the trees. The flicker of heat inside him transformed into a rush of scorching physical response that stiffened his whole body.

Whatever her intentions in wearing that sack, she couldn't have realised it was transparent when backlit by the glaring midday sun. Now he had tantalising glimpses of her long, shapely legs and sultry curves. The flare of her hips and the voluptuous dip to her waist. It was like watching a seductress dancing behind a veil, all that hidden, enticing treasure barely concealed.

His pulse quickened. The camouflage only heightened her body's natural eroticism. So much more effective than the blatant allure of most women he met. Especially as he knew first-hand what treasure she attempted to hide.

Ronan enjoyed every single step of Marina's approach, until she walked into the shadow of the restaurant awning.

Then he settled back in his seat and schooled his features into an expressionless mask.

Marina paused in the shade to draw a steadying breath.

Ronan Carlisle had sounded so certain he had the answer to her problems. Yet surely there *was* no solution. Not after the way she'd stuffed up with Wakefield.

And how could she face Ronan again after last night's debacle? Heat filled her at the memory. Her pride insisted she ignore his summons.

But family duty dictated she attend.

The temptation to turn tail and run was strong. Her inner voice warned Ronan Carlisle was trouble. But she had no choice. She'd meet with the Devil himself if there was any chance to drag her brother out of this mess.

She'd have to brazen it out. Pretend the scene in her bedroom hadn't happened. It was only a kiss, after all. A sensuous, cataclysmic experience for her. But to Ronan Carlisle it probably meant nothing.

She pushed open the restaurant door then stood, eyes adjusting after the brilliant January sunlight. A man at a secluded table instantly captured her attention. He was framed by a pair of French doors that opened onto a picturesque courtyard. The sunlight emphasised the arrogant tilt of his head, the breadth of his shoulders.

Her eyes met his. A jolt of heat held her still. As he looked straight back at her, eyes unreadable, a thrill of something like excitement rippled down her spine.

Or was it apprehension?

Her immediate response to him was too strong, too overwhelming. It scared her.

Drawing herself up straight, she ignored the frantic inner voice urging her to get away, fast. There was too much at stake to turn coward now.

A waitress ushered her across the room. And then Ronan Carlisle was standing. He held out his hand as if this were any other business meeting and he hadn't gathered her close in his arms last night, kissing her till her mind shut down and sensual oblivion beckoned.

A flush spread up her throat and across her cheeks as his hand enveloped hers. Somehow the hard warmth of his hand enclosing hers was appallingly intimate. Deep inside, a quiver of unwanted anticipation trembled into life.

He was just as stunning as she remembered. In tailored linen trousers and a casual blue shirt a few shades lighter than his eyes, he could have graced the cover of an opulent fashion magazine. Editors would pay top dollar for a model like him. That aura of command, with his starkly attractive face and powerful body, made a seductive combination.

'Marina, I'm glad you could make it,' he murmured, his low voice sparking a thrill of reaction through her straining nerves. His expression was bland, but was that a hint of mischief in the curve of his lips?

'Mr Carlisle,' she said, reminding herself that this was business and she had no right to wonder about his smiles. If she kept this formal and pretended nothing had happened between them he'd have to follow suit. 'It's good of you to make time for me.'

Then he did smile, a wide, white, brilliant slash of amusement in his tanned face. 'No need to be so formal.' He squeezed her hand and a corresponding clenching sensation in her chest snagged her breath. 'Call me Ronan.'

'Thanks,' she said, nodding briskly as she withdrew her hand. But she wouldn't take him up on the offer.

His expression reminded her all too vividly of his unnerving stare when he'd walked in to find her ready for bed. And look where that had led!

She sat in the chair he held, and placed her bag beside her. When she swung her head round to face him he was leaning back in his chair, lazily watching her.

His indolence set her teeth on edge and she stiffened. However diverting this might be to him, however foolish she'd been, swooning in his arms, this meeting was important. For her and Seb it meant their whole future.

'How are you feeling today, Marina?'

'Much better, thanks.' The quicker they got off the subject of her health the better. 'You said you had a proposition for me?'

'No need of the crutches today?'

'No.' She stared back at him, but his expression revealed nothing other than polite enquiry. She drew a slow breath, reminding herself that this man might be able to help. No need to go out of her way to antagonise him because she was embarrassed and didn't want to talk about herself. Or because her instincts screamed that he was dangerous.

'I rarely need the crutches now,' she offered. He opened his mouth and she hurried on. Her injuries weren't something she wanted to discuss. 'I was surprised to get your call. I don't understand what you can do to help us.'

One of his sleek dark eyebrows rose, reminding her of the immense power he wielded. If he deigned to help them then maybe there was a chance things would work out.

'Have a little faith, Marina. And in the meantime—' he glanced at the waitress, who'd reappeared beside them '—let's order lunch.'

There was no budging him. As he sat, relaxed and amiable, discussing the menu, and as he made small talk while waiting for their meal, Marina realised this was a man all too used to getting his own way.

He'd invited her to lunch, and lunch they would have. Obviously food was a higher priority than her predicament. Or even last night's explosive embrace.

It took all her patience to sit back and pretend this was a social occasion.

He, on the other hand, was totally at ease. The perfect host, he was solicitous of her comfort, drew her into conversation on general topics and added some amusing anecdotes that made her smile despite her tension.

It wasn't what she'd expected. For an unsettling moment she toyed with the idea that he had another reason for inviting her. That Seb's problem was merely an excuse.

But that was preposterous. Not by look or word had he referred to *that* incident. By mutual consent they'd put it behind them. This was a business meeting.

By the time their seafood meal was served, Marina realised she was ravenous. Last night she'd been too nervous to eat, and this morning it had been tea and toast.

'*Bon appetit,*' he murmured, and lifted his wine glass towards her. Automatically she responded.

His eyes held hers, and this time she couldn't look away. An invisible thread seemed to link them across the small table, drawing them together in a cocoon of intimacy that shut out the muted activity beyond them.

His expression changed, as if some force drew his skin tight over the strong planes and angles of his face. He looked harder, stronger, even more compelling.

Oh, how she remembered that look.

Heat ignited inside her and her palms itched at the temptation he presented. Breathless, she realised she only had to reach out to feel the fine-textured bronze of his flesh, mould the hard line of his jaw.

Even as the insane idea surfaced his eyes widened, almost as if he could read her thoughts. Her pulse skittered. She would *not* be stupid enough to respond that way to him again. She clenched her free hand in her lap and bit down hard on her lip.

'To the success of our plans,' he murmured.

'To a second chance,' she amended, not trusting his expression. It looked like possessiveness. But that was impossible. Her imagination was working overtime.

The white wine was cool and soothing as it slid down her dry throat. She took another sip and nearly sighed with relief as Ronan Carlisle put his glass on the table and dropped his gaze to his plate.

Abruptly the tension that had held her spellbound dissipated. She slumped back in her chair, heart racing as if she'd just swum twenty laps of the pool at top speed.

She needed to get a grip. She'd never had problems concentrating on business. But she'd never had to deal with a man like Ronan Carlisle before. She couldn't let a pair of blue eyes and a handsome face unsettle her.

Fighting the urge to watch him, she turned her attention to the meal. Sooner or later he'd explain this brilliant idea of his.

'I've done some digging since I left you,' he said eventually, 'and I know something of your situation.'

He had her attention now. All of it.

'But I need to know more.'

'You said you knew how we can get the firm back.'

He nodded. 'All in good time. First I want to make sure I understand the circumstances completely. My contacts could only provide so much information for me last night.'

'You rang them last *night?*' It must have been nearly midnight by the time he'd left her.

'Not all work is conducted between nine and five,' he said, as if the middle of the night was a perfectly reasonable time to call business contacts.

She shook her head, wondering about the urgency of his actions. But that didn't matter. All that mattered was the fact that he was willing to help.

'What do you know?'

'That our friend Wakefield is in the process of acquiring another company to add to his portfolio. A medium-sized and quite profitable freight company.' His eyes bored into hers. 'Marina Enterprises. It's owned by a family called Lucchesi.'

She laid her cutlery on the plate carefully, as if it was important it shouldn't fall and clatter.

'That's right,' she said flatly. 'My father started the firm. Built it up from nothing.' She twisted the stem of her wine goblet between her fingers. 'But it's jointly owned by my brother Sebastian and me.' She drew a deep breath. 'Or it was.'

'Until Charles Wakefield came on the scene.' She thought she heard the echo of sympathy in his deep voice.

She pushed back her shoulders and took a sip of the crisp wine he'd ordered. She didn't need sympathy. She needed action.

'Seb owes Wakefield a lot of money,' she said brusquely. 'The company was security for a debt, and Wakefield's demanding payment in full. Immediately. Legally, he's within his rights.' She swallowed down the bitter taste of nausea at the injustice of it and forced the words out. 'Seb's tried everything to raise the money, but he can't get his hands on that sort of cash.'

'So Wakefield gets the company.'

'I don't see what you can do about it,' she burst out. 'I thought if I met Wakefield I might be able to persuade him to give us more time. We could look at a loan, sell some of the firm's assets.'

Never mind that it would gut the company and they'd never recover financially.

'But he'll never agree to it now. Not after what I said to him.' She shuddered. Her stomach churned at the memory of last night's disaster. She couldn't have done a better job of sabotaging any last chance to reason with Wakefield if she'd tried.

She couldn't believe how easily that slimeball had got to her. All because she'd been tired and stressed. That was no excuse. She should have done better. Should have found a way past his arrogance and her own stupid pride.

Just as well her parents weren't around to see how badly she and Seb had mismanaged their legacy. It would have broken their hearts. She blinked furiously as her eyes blurred and pain radiated from that inner well of grief.

'Slow down, Marina.' He reached out and covered her hand, where it fisted on the pristine linen cloth. His touch was warmth and reassurance. And something else. Something that made her flesh tingle beneath his palm. But she knew the contact meant nothing to him.

'Tell me what happened.'

Her lips pursed at the thought of laying bare Seb's naïve stupidity to this man who dealt in billion-dollar deals. She tried to pull her hand out from under his.

He wouldn't release her. No fuss, no pain, but his hold was unbreakable. Just like the intensity of his stare.

'Tell me,' he urged.

She looked at his square hand engulfing hers. It made her own look almost dainty, her wrist slender and feminine. And it warmed her in a way that made her hot all over.

Damn, but she didn't like this. It felt all wrong.

'Dad was grooming Seb to take his role as head of the company,' she said at last.

'And you?'

She lifted her face to find him leaning close, so close she could see tiny flecks of azure in his dark eyes and inhale his clean, spicy scent. Something clogged in her brain, and for long moments she stared at him, unable to concentrate on anything else. Dimly she was aware of her clamouring senses, of her racing heartbeat.

Her eyes dropped to his sculpted lips. A surge of longing engulfed her.

For God's sake, concentrate!

She straightened in her seat. 'I'm a qualified accountant. I work in the firm's financial team and I'm a company director.' No need to tell him she'd been co-running the company for the last year or so with her dad.

'My father died several months ago in a car accident.' Her tone was matter-of-fact, giving nothing away. But his hand tightened round hers, squeezing warmth into her suddenly chilled flesh.

'And you were injured in the same accident.' It wasn't a

question. His gaze was sharp. 'Tell me, just how long ago did you get out of hospital?'

'That's hardly relevant.'

'Humour me,' he said softly, as his thumb stroked tantalisingly over her knuckles.

The tiny movement created a lush wave of seductive warmth that spread across her hand, over her wrist and up her arm. Some of her brittle defences shattered.

'I moved out of physical rehabilitation two weeks ago.'

She watched anger add brilliance to his glittering eyes. 'And I can take care of myself.' As if it was any of his business. 'I've looked after Dad and Seb since I was thirteen.'

'And now who's looking after you?'

Furious, she yanked her hand away. This time he released it, and she tucked it safely in her lap, steadfastly ignoring the way it tingled from his caress.

'I'm perfectly fine on my own. And Seb can't be at my beck and call. He has a new bride.'

'Married at twenty-one?'

He must have a phenomenal memory to recall that from last night's barrage of accusations.

She shrugged. 'They were in love.' And, her father had assured her, marriage to Emma was just what Seb needed to help him settle down.

Absently she rubbed a finger over her right hand, as if she could erase the lingering sensation of his touch.

'I don't see why you need to know all this.'

'Because I like to know what I'm getting into,' he countered, and the look he gave her was all business. Only an unwise woman would argue now. The angle of his jaw and the steely glint in his eye belonged to the wealthy corporate powerbroker, not the charming lunch partner. Nor the passionate lover who'd almost seduced her twelve hours ago.

'So,' he recapped, 'you and your younger brother jointly own Marina Enterprises. And…?'

'Dad was gone, and I was stuck in hospital.' She leaned back in her chair, suddenly exhausted. She stared out into the courtyard. A soothing trickle of water splashed from a wall fountain into a pool surrounded by ferns.

'My brother was eager to make his mark. He wanted to prove himself.' Their dad was a hard act to follow. But she'd never realised how much Seb felt he had to show himself his father's equal.

'Even before the accident he'd been working on plans to expand the firm. He'd made some new contacts and talked about borrowing to diversify while the market was right. It would be a good scheme, so long as he did it properly.'

'But he didn't.' It wasn't a question but a grim pronouncement.

She shook her head, feeling once more that swooping feeling in the pit of her stomach, the nauseous horror at the enormity of Seb's stupidity.

'Some of his new business contacts were extremely successful and had plenty of disposable income. There were weekend-long parties and gambling for high stakes. Seb got invited to a few.' She still wondered about that. Couldn't understand why Seb, handsome and ambitious as he was, had been welcomed so readily into that *milieu*.

'Charles Wakefield hosted a racing party,' she said, eager now to get this over. 'Emma was away, so Seb went alone. He gambled till he'd lost all he could afford, but Wakefield persuaded him to stay on. Later, after Seb had been drinking far too much, Wakefield mentioned how easy it would be to raise the money for the expansion if he had one good win, rather than bother with a bank loan.'

She took a ragged breath and plunged on. 'Seb knew he had no more money to bet, but Wakefield assured him it was all right. Said something about a gentlemen's agreement.' And in his sozzled state Seb had actually believed him!

'My brother lost. And the next day Wakefield told him he'd signed over the company as security.'

'It was definitely his signature?' Ronan Carlisle leaned close across the table, his only sign of animation.

Marina nodded, reliving the sickening moment of revelation. 'Oh, yes, it was his.' Her voice was bitter. 'Wakefield didn't leave anything to chance. One of his lawyers just happened to be on hand to witness it. The document is legally binding—we've checked. And Wakefield had witnesses there to testify that Seb knew what he was doing when he signed it.'

'Greedy bastard.' Ronan Carlisle sat back and rubbed a hand over his jaw.

'Precisely.'

Looking down, she saw the scraps of her meal, cold on her plate. She shuddered and pushed it away. If only this had all been a bad dream.

'But you own the company jointly. Your brother couldn't sign away what wasn't his.'

'And what would you have me do?' she demanded on a surge of fury. 'Watch him struggle with a debt he'll never be able to pay? Have him blacklisted by every potential future employer and finance company because of bankruptcy?'

She sank back in her chair and regarded him wearily. Every bone in her body ached with tiredness. She was so close to giving up the fight that it scared her.

'He bet the company and more besides. Wakefield won't accept any alternative.'

'So you're selling your family home to help?'

'How did you—?'

'I drove you home last night, remember? There was a real estate agent's sign on the footpath.' He paused. 'Where will you live?'

Marina stared. What did it matter where she lived? She'd just returned home after the shock of her father's death and months in hospital. She hadn't even been able to attend her dad's funeral, and for a while there she'd thought she'd never overcome her grief. But then she'd discovered her family company was as good as in a stranger's hands. Everything her parents had worked towards all their lives.

Right now nothing else mattered. Not even her frighteningly intense feelings for this man.

'I'll worry about that when the time comes. You said you knew what we could do to keep the company,' she challenged, waiting for him to prevaricate.

Instead he returned her gaze, unblinking and confident.

Whatever he had in mind, he was sure he could bring it off. Certainty was there in his relaxed posture, and in the tiny smile that curved his sculpted lips.

'You *do* have a plan, don't you?' Excitement stirred.

He inclined his head. 'It's unorthodox.'

She sat back in her chair, wondering exactly what that meant. 'Illegal? Is that it?' she asked suspiciously.

His lips twitched and she watched, mesmerised. Did he have any idea just how sexy that made him look?

'No. I may be creative in my approach to business, but I always stay on the right side of the law.'

Absently she nodded, aware of his reputation not only for success, but for fair dealing. The corporate regulators never had problems with Ronan Carlisle's companies.

So what was his plan? And why was he bothering? Marina Enterprises was a solidly successful company and worth saving. But what was in it for him?

Her earlier unease returned. She knew where she stood with Wakefield. He was a womaniser, a louse and a cheat.

But Ronan Carlisle? She knew his public reputation as rich, innovative and successful. She'd learned last night that he was determined, confident and surprisingly considerate for a mega-wealthy tycoon. And that his shuttered expression hid a passionate, incredibly sensual nature. That he kissed with the expertise and ruthless eroticism of a fallen angel.

And now he knew so much about her. He'd delved into her personal life and stripped her bare of all defences. She felt totally vulnerable.

'Why are you getting involved?' she asked breathlessly.

Again that half-smile that made her heart somersault. He leaned towards her. The scent of him assailed her, clean and male and provocative.

'You and your brother aren't the only ones to suffer at Wakefield's hands.'

He was silent for a moment, as if choosing his words. 'He can be dangerous when he wants something, and the results can be disastrous.'

The grooves bracketing his mouth deepened as his lips compressed. A flash of raw emotion burned in his eyes.

Pain? Marina was an expert at recognising it. After all, she'd seen it for so long now, reflected back if ever she looked in the mirror.

'So you want revenge?' she said.

There was no discernible change in his expression, but he looked so uncompromising, so far removed from her urbane lunch companion, it sent a chill through her. She had no difficulty believing he could be totally ruthless in getting whatever he set his heart on. No matter what the opposition. Or the cost.

'Perhaps,' he answered. 'But, more important, I want Wakefield so busy working to keep his head above water that he won't have time to destroy anyone else.'

Destroy. It was a strong word. But that was what Wakefield was doing. Destroying Seb's future and her own. Stealing her father's hard-won legacy.

She nodded, steadfastly ignoring the aura of danger emanating from Ronan Carlisle. Hadn't she decided she'd do a deal even with the Devil if she had to?

'What do you have in mind?'

He sat back and watched her through narrowed eyes. 'It will only work with your co-operation,' he warned.

'All right. You need me and my brother.'

'No.' He didn't raise his voice, but the single syllable cut across her jumble of thoughts. 'Not your brother. Just you.'

Marina's pulse thudded, slow and heavy, compounding the dull roar in her ears. All her senses were on alert, as if she was an animal stalked by a predator, on the lookout for certain attack.

This smelt like danger. It felt like impending catastrophe. But she couldn't pull back.

'What do I have to do?'

The grooves beside his mouth folded deeper, not with humour this time, but with satisfaction.

'I want you to become my mistress.'

CHAPTER SIX

MARINA jerked back as if she'd been slapped. What sort of game was he playing?

He met her stunned look with arrogant assurance.

For a moment she even wondered if she'd heard him right. Then her chair scraped across the polished wood floor as she shoved it back.

But the way he sat there, calm and unruffled, goaded her. Instead of thrusting up out of her seat she leaned across the table, the full blaze of her fury and hurt consuming her. She might have made a fool of herself when he kissed her, but she didn't deserve this.

'If that's your attempt at humour, I don't think it's funny.'

No response. Only the steady regard of hooded eyes scrutinising her like a beetle under a microscope.

'And if it's a reference to what happened last night…' She slammed a lid on the memory of his body against hers, his lips so utterly persuasive. 'You can be sure there'll never be a repeat performance.'

Not even to herself would she admit how much she'd wanted to trust Ronan Carlisle. The realisation of her mistake was a raw, scalding ache deep inside, making it hard to breathe.

'This isn't about last night, Marina, delightful as that was.' His voice was as smooth and seductive as rich chocolate, and a responsive thrill of pleasure skated through her body, stoking her anger.

She glared into his indigo eyes, trying to discern his expression, but it was shuttered. All she had were his words.

'My proposal is unorthodox, but it *will* work. I'll get you back your company…if you co-operate with me.'

'Yeah, sure. Me as your mistress. I can see that!'

'Why not?' He leaned towards her across the small table so their faces were only a breath apart.

Furious, she registered her body's response to him: tingling awareness, a telltale flush of heat. And she despised herself for it.

'Your boyfriend would object? Is that the problem?'

She swung away, but his hand closed over hers, clamping it uncompromisingly to the table.

She tugged, but her strength was no match for his. He didn't even seem to exert any pressure—to an onlooker his touch would seem intimate, not imprisoning.

'Let me go,' she snarled.

'In a moment. After you tell me why it wouldn't work.' He paused, his gaze raking her face. 'Is it because there's some man in your life? A lover?'

She shook her head.

'So what's the problem?'

'First,' she spat out, 'your sex-life has nothing to do with Charles Wakefield, and it's not going to get back Marina Enterprises. And second, it's just ridiculous.'

His eyebrows slanted up. 'Why is it ridiculous?'

'I've had enough now. Let me go.'

'After you explain.'

She tried to prise her hand from under his, but he refused to release her and she couldn't break his hold. His ability to keep her there was the final straw. She had enough arrogant men in her life. She'd be damned if she'd put up with another one.

'I'm not mistress material. Anyone can see that.' If she had been, maybe he wouldn't have found it so easy to walk away from her last night. A shaft of burning pain pierced her. She knew her limitations.

'On the contrary,' he said, his voice so low and sensuous that she shivered. 'I can see you in the role.'

Marina sucked in a breath at the image he evoked in her wayward imagination. Her and this man. Together. Intimate.

Something inside her melted into swirling sensation at the thought of it. Her nipples peaked and moist heat welled low in her body as she remembered how close they'd come to being lovers.

'I'm sorry I didn't make it clear, Marina,' he said softly. 'I should have said *pretend* to be my mistress.'

Pretend?

She stared, trying to make sense of his words.

'If we can convince Wakefield that we're involved,' he murmured, 'it will create the opportunity I need. With you as bait I can entice him so far out on a limb that releasing Marina Enterprises to your family will be the least of his worries.'

His words fell like a pledge into the silence. He was serious now, both face and voice grim.

He really meant it!

Her mind boggled. His suggestion that she pose as anyone's mistress was in the worst possible taste.

Marina shook her head. 'I wouldn't be convincing.' Not if she had to play the role of *femme fatale.* The whole idea was ludicrous, cruelly so. 'Whatever you have in mind, it won't work.'

'Of course it will work. Can't you find it in yourself to trust me, even a little?' His lips quirked in a half-smile that she was sure he'd practised on countless gullible females.

She took a slow breath and marshalled her thoughts, tried to calm her pounding heart. Saving her family company. That was what counted. She should hear him out.

'Not trust,' she said, surprised at how steady her voice sounded. 'But I'll listen.'

'Good.' His hand slid back, releasing hers. To her dismay she missed the lingering warmth of his touch.

'We'll go somewhere more private to discuss it.' He stood and tucked a hand under her elbow.

In anyone else she would have thought the gesture merely solicitous, especially after her physical weakness last night. But to her dazed mind his touch against her bare skin felt like a brand of ownership. She shivered.

* * *

'You were going to explain,' she prompted as they sat in her living room. He turned his gaze from the family photos covering one wall and watched her with those unreadable eyes. Uncomfortable under his scrutiny, she steeled herself to remain motionless, apparently at ease.

'I decided to act against Wakefield some time ago.' Ronan's voice was dispassionate. 'He's extended his personal resources recklessly in the last year, grabbing at opportunities but not consolidating. Despite his wealth, that leaves him vulnerable. A single major loss at the wrong time would leave him desperate.'

His lips curved, easing the stark lines of his face. But it was a predatory smile with a ruthless edge. When he looked like that Ronan Carlisle scared her. Something Wakefield, for all his money, had never managed.

'I need a diversion to preoccupy him while I spring the trap.' His gaze held hers. 'That's where you come in.'

Marina tried to ignore the flare of heated awareness his obvious approval evoked and concentrate on the facts. 'I still don't understand.'

He stretched his long legs towards her. She felt the brush of his shoe against her sandalled foot and shifted uneasily.

'You're perfect,' he said, his voice a low purr of satisfaction that made the hairs on her arms rise. His eyes were warm as they rested on her. 'You have reason to hate Wakefield, so you won't fall victim to his charm.'

'Charm?' Her voice rose in amazement. 'That snake has as much charm as a tax auditor.'

'You're judging him with the benefit of inside knowledge. He's handsome and rich, and, believe me, he can convince most women he's the man of their dreams.'

'Not this woman!'

'That's exactly why I need you.'

Ronan held her bewildered gaze. She sat forward in her chair, luminous eyes fixed on him and lips slightly parted. A surge of exultant heat filled him.

She was like some seductive earth goddess, hiding herself

beneath a prim hairstyle and shapeless, sexless clothes. But she couldn't conceal the passion, the voluptuous femininity he'd discovered in her. The memory of her mouth alone had been enough to keep him awake into the early hours. And that body…

Why was she so adamant she couldn't pretend to be his mistress? He could imagine it so clearly he was burning up. But she acted as if she didn't have beauty on her side, or intelligence. Or the innate sensuality that drew him irresistibly to her.

Yet she was born for the role.

All he had to do was get her to admit it.

He was sorely tempted to throw common sense to the winds. To lean over right now and skim his fingers over the tender flesh of her cheek. To release the vibrant luxury of her long hair so it caressed him as he claimed the softness of her flagrantly erotic mouth with his own, fast and hard.

Heat pooled in his belly.

It would be a mistake. Reason was an ice-cold douche to his fervid imaginings. Instead he contented himself with the promise that one day soon the time would be right.

One day very soon.

He had plans for Marina. Plans he had no intention of revealing yet.

In the meantime there was still much to do. First he had to assuage her doubts. He didn't share his feelings easily, and dredging up the past held no appeal. But it was necessary if he was to convince her.

'Wakefield is dangerous,' he said. 'He's hurt too many people and he needs to be stopped before he ruins any more lives.' He paused, deciding how much he needed to reveal.

'We met at boarding school,' he continued eventually, his voice clipped. 'Wakefield's father and grandfather were old boys there. But I was the son of an entrepreneur; Dad started from nothing. Wakefield thought that made us second rate, but I was proud of my father. Still am.'

He saw a glimmer of understanding in Marina's face, a nod of approval. So that explained her fierce determination to wrest her birthright back from Wakefield. If her father had been her hero, then guilt at the loss of his company drove her on as much as a desire for justice.

'Wakefield never took to me. He lorded it over his cronies but I wouldn't kowtow to him. He tried to make school hell, but I refused to leave. He even tried to thrash me once, but he didn't manage it.' Ronan looked into Marina's wide-eyed gaze, reading surprise there, and something he couldn't identify. Distaste?

'After that we were rivals in everything: studies, sport, you name it.' He paused, remembering Wakefield's brutal methods—anything to win. Wakefield had been a vicious young thug, and the years hadn't improved him.

'And then, in our final year, there was a girl.'

'Your girl?' she interrupted, her dark eyes probing.

'No, his. He broke up with her. She was upset, not him. He was too busy bragging about—' Ronan shot Marina a piercing look. Her expression told him she got the picture.

'Her brother was a mate of mine. But Charlie-boy decided there was something between me and her. He didn't want her, but he didn't want me to have her. He warned me off.' He shrugged. 'When I ignored him he turned nasty. He couldn't hurt her, or me. But there was her kid brother. They found him one night, beaten and bleeding.'

Marina's hiss of indrawn breath was loud, and he nodded. He remembered vividly his own horror the night they'd carted Simon off to hospital. And his rage.

'He claimed not to have recognised his attacker. But Wakefield made sure I knew he'd done it. When there weren't any witnesses around, of course.'

'You're joking!' she gasped. 'He'd have to be mad.'

He inclined his head. 'Definitely unhinged when he's crossed.' A pity the bastard hadn't been forced to get professional help years ago. That might have prevented him inflicting so much damage on innocents.

Silence filled the room as she absorbed his story. She hunched in her chair, arms wrapped protectively round herself.

Good. It was time she realised how dangerous Wakefield could be. The way she'd stood up to him last night had filled

Ronan with admiration, but it was clear she hadn't realised the man was an unprincipled lout.

'We've had little direct contact until recently.' He wrested his attention back to the present. 'But lately, for a number of reasons, I've kept a close eye on him. Even attended one or two of his functions. Our commercial interests are in different spheres. Or they were. In the last twelve months he's been sniffing at my heels, trying to expand into the transport industry.'

Ronan's business empire had been built from a base in international air freight. And he had no doubt that was precisely where Charlie would like to diversify.

Her eyes narrowed as she realised the significance of his words. He'd been right. Marina was no one's fool.

'You've made the connection.' He nodded. 'It's not coincidence that he wants Marina Enterprises. He'd like to become a serious competitor.'

'And that bothers you?' she asked, brows arching.

He shook his head, relishing the idea of an up-front battle. 'Let him bring it on. I'd be fascinated to see how well he manages in a field other than commercial property.'

Marina frowned, and he saw the inevitable question in her gaze. 'There's more, isn't there?' she asked.

As he'd thought: definitely an intelligent woman.

Yet he hesitated. Could he risk revealing the truth to this woman who, essentially, was a stranger? Would she keep it to herself or try to use it for gain?

He stared at her through narrowed eyes, wondering if she was as innocent as she seemed. Whether this morning's lightning-fast security assessment was reliable. Was she indeed principled and talented, as well as hard-working and supremely unlucky? His gut instinct urged him to trust her.

But if he was wrong… No, he couldn't take that chance. This was Cleo's life. Not ancient history from his school days. And she'd worked so hard to claw her way back towards regaining what she'd lost. He couldn't risk it. If the truth leaked out it would destroy her.

He surged to his feet, striding to the window and swinging

round to face Marina. Tension throbbed across his shoulders and up his neck, holding him rigid.

'Wakefield hurt someone I care for. Hurt them badly.' He paused. 'I don't want them hurt again.'

'I don't gossip.' Her voice was matter-of-fact. 'But if there's more to know about Charles Wakefield I'd like to hear it. Forewarned is forearmed.'

The acrid taste of guilt seared his mouth. If only he'd warned Cleo… If only he'd suspected the lengths that twisted bastard would go to with his sick games.

And here was another of his victims. He looked into Marina's lustrous eyes, read concern in her furrowed brow, and knew a surge of protectiveness so strong it rocked him.

'I can't tell you the specifics. It's not my story. But I can tell you to watch out, because Wakefield will use *any* tactic to get what he wants. And what happened to my…friend was done deliberately. The only reason he targeted her was because of her link to me.'

He shoved his hands deep in his pockets. 'It sounds melodramatic, but what started as a schoolboy rivalry has become a dangerous obsession. Wakefield is fixated on besting me any way he can.'

'I…see. But where do I come in?'

He doubted if she did see. But she was listening.

'Wakefield's reputation as a ladies' man is well deserved,' he said brusquely. 'And that's his weakness. One of the few things that can distract him from making money.'

She nodded. Wakefield's playboy reputation was public knowledge.

'In the last few years he's taken a particular interest in the women I've dated. Occasionally dated some of them himself later on. It's happened often enough for it to be no coincidence. A few have even complained that he was too persistent, virtually stalking them.'

Marina's confusion was obvious from her knitted brow.

'His marked interest in them, like his new interest in freight, tells me that the old rivalry is still alive in his mind. He's so predictable it's almost laughable.' Except for the fact that people were getting hurt again.

He watched Marina, hands clasped as if in prayer, her face like a luminous Madonna's. That sack of a dress only hinted at her sensuous curves, making her look like a temptress hiding in a nun's habit.

He needed her. Badly. But he had to tread warily.

He swung away from her dark questioning eyes.

Marina stared at those wide shoulders, hunched as if against the cold. Or with the strain of painful memories.

This tale of a jealous rival was so far-fetched. She could hardly credit it. In any other circumstances she wouldn't believe it. But she had the evidence of Ronan Carlisle's voice, his body, his torment, to convince her.

No one was that good an actor.

His pain was so intense, so raw, it vibrated from him in waves. And the flare of hatred in his eyes when he'd blamed Wakefield had been truly terrible. She wondered if Wakefield understood the force he'd unleashed when he'd hurt Ronan Carlisle's girlfriend.

For she had to be his lover, not a mere friend. The anguish in his eyes had been so absolute.

'He's destroying people,' Ronan said at last. 'But I'm his real target, so I'm the one who has to end it.'

He paused, turning to meet her gaze in a way that made heat rise in her throat. 'Wakefield will sit up and take notice if he thinks you're mine.' The heat spread to her cheeks, and down much, much lower.

'His competitive instinct won't let him rest. He'll try to win you for himself. And while he's chasing you he won't be concentrating on business.'

'But he looked at me as if I'd crawled out from under a stone!' Her voice rose to a protesting squeak and she cleared her throat. 'No way would he chase after *me.*'

'You underestimate yourself,' he assured her, his eyes holding hers. 'And you underestimate his egomania. He believes he can get any woman he wants. The harder the chase, the more important it is for him to win.'

'You didn't see the way he looked at me. I embarrassed him at his party. He's not going to see me as a trophy!'

'I know Wakefield,' he said, and the confidence in his voice had the ring of truth. 'If he thinks you're mine he'll try to seduce you away. Your confrontation with him won't matter if he thinks there's a chance to best me.'

She shook her head. Why couldn't Ronan Carlisle see what was in front of his nose? He was so set on revenge that he was blind to the obvious.

'You need someone glamorous,' she said eventually, ignoring her outraged pride. 'You need someone who *looks* like they might be your mistress.' *Someone with the experience to carry it off.* It was only sheer determination that allowed her to meet his eyes.

'And you don't?'

She kept her lips firmly closed, refusing to answer.

He stared back at her. 'What if I said you were wrong? That I like women with fire and passion, who stand up for what they believe in no matter what the odds?'

For a moment her heart stopped. She so wanted to believe him. But she wasn't into fantasy. This wouldn't work.

'I don't look like anyone's mistress,' she repeated.

'Clothes,' he said dismissively. 'That's soon fixed. You need something sensational. Not that suit you wore last night.'

'There's nothing wrong with my suit.' It was comfortable, and perfectly respectable.

'Except it's a couple of sizes too large. It conceals too much.'

'And maybe I want to be concealed.'

He shook his head and paced across the room to her. She had to tilt her head up to meet his gaze, the strain in her neck making her feel even more vulnerable.

'Most women with a body like the one I saw last night would happily flaunt it. I'm sure you could manage it for a few weeks. To save your brother.'

Her jaw sagged as she heard his words. A body worth flaunting? She blinked and stared. Had she heard him right?

'But I'm too…' Her voice trailed off under his scrutiny. 'Too tall,' she finished lamely. No way could she bring herself to use any of the other labels: big, buxom, oversized.

'Too tall.' He sat down opposite her and leaned back. His rigid control drained away as his mouth curved into a smile that creased his face, stunning her with its vibrancy. He laughed, and the sound, rich and mellow, melted the hard knot of unhappiness deep within her.

'I'm hardly in miniature myself,' he said at last. 'I'd look ridiculous with a tiny woman on my arm. My women are always tall.'

Marina swallowed hard at the thought of being included in the list of his women.

If things had been different last night…

'But Wakefield's only my height,' she said, as if it really mattered. As if it were even possible that a handsome multi-millionaire would give her a second look.

Ronan Carlisle's eyes gleamed. 'Don't you know lots of men fantasise about tall women? Buy the highest stilettos you can find. You'll have him drooling in no time.'

She shook her head, denying the ridiculous ideas that filled it. Her dressed to kill. Her as a sexy vamp, playing off one wealthy tycoon against the other.

If it weren't so pathetic she'd laugh. Ronan had had no difficulty keeping his distance from her, even though she'd all but offered herself to him on a platter. She cringed. Oh, no, her *charms* definitely weren't up to the role.

Her eyes strayed across the room to the photos on the wall. Her mother looked out of the central one, her smile brilliant and alluring. She was dressed for a party, her pocket-Venus curves emphasised by the gorgeous cocktail dress she wore. Now, *there* was a beautiful woman.

'It's all academic anyway,' she said harshly. 'Even if I could lure Wakefield's attention away from business for a short time, that won't get the company back for us.'

Ronan Carlisle watched her silently for so long she shifted in her seat, wondering how much of her inner turmoil he sensed.

'You're wrong. I've worked towards this. I know how precarious Wakefield's cash flow is. He's overstretched. Which is probably why he used such desperate measures to grab your company.' Ronan leaned back and crossed one ankle over the other, the picture of male confidence.

'I've got a deal coming up that will put him just where I want him. He'll think it's the opportunity of a lifetime to catch me unprepared. And when he reacts, tries to get the better of me by grabbing first for another company, he'll overreach the mark. That's when I'll reel him in, and call in a few of his debts.'

His face glowed with savage satisfaction. His grin looked carnivorous, and Marina experienced a fleeting pang of sympathy for his enemy. Ronan Carlisle wouldn't show any mercy to the man who'd hurt his woman.

'The timing's perfect,' he continued. 'With your help we can get Wakefield where it will hurt most: his ego and his hip pocket. I can engineer it so he surrenders Marina Enterprises. You and your brother will be shot of Wakefield *and* the debt if you help me.'

He made it sound easy. Too easy. She knew nothing in life was that simple. Such multi-company dealings were far more complex and risky than he'd described.

She stared across at the man who had taken over her life in one short day. Who did she think she was kidding, even pretending she could play in his league? She was a minnow who'd unwittingly ventured among barracudas.

And even though he understood Wakefield, and could no doubt manage a hostile takeover bid as easily as she did a bowl of steaming pasta, Ronan Carlisle had miscalculated.

She wasn't the sort of woman men burned for. She'd never even had a serious boyfriend. What did she know about tempting a man?

'I'm sorry,' she said at last, squashing a pang of regret. 'This isn't going to work.'

Hours later, and still Ronan Carlisle's words played in her ears. His presence haunted her. She paced the bedroom, too wide awake to sleep, her thoughts tumbling over each other as she racked her brain for a way out of this mess.

She halted at the mirror tucked behind the door, her attention caught by her outrageous mop of curls. She should cut her hair.

With her father gone no one would complain if she did. She pulled the locks away from her face.

She looked different since the accident. Her cheekbones were more defined, the curve of her lips more pronounced. She frowned. Or maybe she was just getting older and she'd never bothered to look properly before.

Mirrors had never been her favourite thing. Not since she'd turned thirteen and developed womanly curves before all the other girls. It took confidence to carry off a figure like that so young, and she hadn't had it. Not then. And especially not after her mother's death in the same year.

Marina had taken refuge in the kitchen, comfort-eating and trying to take her mum's place there, organising the family. And after that it had been easy to slip into the habit: focus on study and work and family. Ignore the jibes of slim, sexy, confident girls who had no idea there was anything more important in life than their next boyfriend. Not worry about frivolous things like parties and fashion.

Marina's gaze strayed down over her silk nightgown, wondering how Ronan Carlisle had seen her the night before. Her hands smoothed the sensuous fabric over her stomach and hips, down across her thighs, remembering his touch.

He was right. She stepped closer to the glass, peering at her outline. The curves of her bust and hips were still there, nothing could take those away, but they were sleek, streamlined, with none of the excess she'd so dreaded in the past.

One of the benefits of a stint in physical rehabilitation. Sensible eating and exercise to get her legs working again.

The phone rang and she scowled. Who'd ring so late?

Fifteen minutes later she hung up, feeling dazed. Could life throw any more curve balls?

The looming loss of the company had brought Seb to his senses. He'd worked night and day, trying to find a way to stop Wakefield's takeover. He'd matured, realising his responsibility to his family, and to his employees. But clearly today's news had unnerved him.

She sat motionless, wondering what to do. Her glance fell on the plain business card resting on her bedside table. Ronan Carlisle had insisted she take his private number in case she changed her mind.

One slow breath. Then another.

Had she changed her mind?

It didn't matter whether she had or not. Not with Seb's news that they weren't the only ones losing their inheritance. Not with the news that Emma was pregnant.

She knew what her father would have done: whatever it took to secure the firm for the next generation. She faced the truth now, with a sense of leaden detachment. They had one chance only to retrieve their birthright.

She reached out a hand and grabbed the phone, refusing to stop and think about what she was doing.

He answered almost immediately. 'Carlisle.' Just that, in a voice that even at this distance created a dangerous whirlpool of need and longing deep inside her.

She was going to regret this, she knew. But she didn't have the luxury of choice.

'It's me,' she whispered. 'Marina Lucchesi. I've changed my mind.'

CHAPTER SEVEN

'AREN'T they a bit much? Too extreme?' Marina asked, as she turned to peer down at the four-inch stiletto heels.

The dressy sandals had the narrowest of diamanté-studded black straps across her toes, and pairs of shoestring ribbons that curled up around her ankles to tie on her legs.

'You've got to be kidding,' Bella Montrose said in her smoky drawl. She leaned forward in one of the boutique's exclusive designer armchairs for a better view. 'Dynamite is what you want, honey, and that's exactly what you've got there.'

Marina looked at the elegant personal stylist who'd been her companion for the past three days. Ever since Ronan Carlisle had rung and announced she'd be arriving at nine a.m. sharp to oversee Marina's transformation.

The arrogance of his announcement still rankled. Almost as much as his calm acceptance when Marina had changed her mind and agreed to this charade. As if there'd never been any doubt that she'd agree to do what he wanted.

'Well?' Bella raised one artfully sleek eyebrow, returning Marina's look with what might, in a less refined woman, be a grin of self-satisfaction. 'You know you love them. You're just being obstinate again.'

'If I might say,' chimed in the saleswoman, 'for a special evening they *are* the most stunning shoe we have. The straps draw attention to the lovely curve of your leg.'

Marina twisted her foot and stared at the full-length mirror.

It was true they were unlike any shoes she'd worn before. In height, price and sexiness. She'd been afraid she'd look like a tart, or, worse, a clown, in sandals so outrageously provocative. But her feet were well-shaped, something she'd never appreciated before. Her ankles were trim and her calves did look…feminine.

Even wearing her favourite loose summer dress, the one Bella had threatened to burn, she looked different in these shoes. As if she might be a seductress in disguise.

She almost laughed out loud at the absurdity. But then, as so often today, her eyes lifted again to the reflection of her newly trimmed and treated hair.

What a transformation. The hours at the expensive salon had been worth every minute. She still didn't understand the intricacies of what the team of stylists had done. But the result bore no resemblance to the untameable mop she'd started with. Her curls had been persuaded into lush waves that flowed invitingly over her shoulders and framed her face perfectly.

Even her hands looked different, more feminine, with their elegantly shaped and painted nails.

She blinked.

Was that really her in the mirror?

'I'll take them,' she said on impulse. Maybe the sandals went with her new image after all. Or maybe she'd just given up a lifetime's habit of choosing sensible over glamorous.

With Bella, she was almost learning to enjoy shopping.

'And she'll take the red ones as well,' Bella said.

Marina opened her mouth to protest, then caught the older woman's eye. Bella was right; the red would be perfect with the outfit they'd bought earlier. Even Marina, with her inexperienced eye, could see that.

Though after three whole days with Bella, Marina couldn't claim any longer to be untutored in the secrets of fashion. They'd discussed colour, body shape, face shape, dress design, jewellery, posture—though apparently she had no problems there—and make-up.

She'd been bullied into hundreds—or was it thousands?—of outfits, until eventually she'd understood why Bella so emphatically approved of some clothes and shuddered at others.

Forced to look in the mirror again and again, she could see now that the cover-up dresses she wore did her no favours, while some of the styles she'd avoided were almost flattering.

She'd even let herself be talked into new underwear that was silky, seductive and utterly decadent. She'd insisted it was unnecessary, had almost blurted out that no one else would see it. But Bella had been adamant that she needed a makeover from the skin out.

And Bella knew what she was talking about. The delicate caress of silk against Marina's body did make her feel…different. Not like her old self at all.

By the time they'd made it to the discreet salon this morning, Marina had been eager to have her hair cut short, ready to embrace a whole new image. Even the chief hairstylist's disapproval hadn't dimmed her enthusiasm. It had taken Bella's throaty murmur, stating that Ronan had specifically ordered her hair be kept long, to stop her. After all, he was financing this masquerade.

But it had stuck in her craw—him dictating something as intimate as the way she wore her hair. She'd been tempted to ignore his wishes and suit herself. Yet she'd known as soon as she saw the results that he'd been right.

Blast the man! How had he known? And, more to the point, why had he even bothered to think of it? Surely the length of her hair was a trivial detail.

She sat down and took off the delicate sandals. They were so fragile, so extravagant. So not like her.

A pang of misgiving speared her. Would this plan of Ronan's work? Could she really snare Charles Wakefield's interest and hold it long enough to distract him even a little from his business?

She shook her head at the ridiculous notion. A change of clothes couldn't make that much difference. She was still essentially the same: too lacking in feminine wiles, too scarred to attract a man. She had about as much sex appeal as double-entry bookkeeping.

Then she looked up and caught sight of the stranger in the mirror. She didn't look like herself any more.

A discreet chirrup interrupted her reverie, and she watched Bella flip open her silver cellphone.

'Ronan!' There was genuine delight in the other woman's voice.

Immediately Marina tensed. It was nonsensical, but just a call from Ronan Carlisle was enough to disrupt her equilibrium. He'd burst into her life like a hurricane, turning everything topsy-turvy. Nothing was like it had been before. And she had a sinking premonition that *she* would never be the same again.

She bent over and concentrated on slipping on her flat sandals.

'Sure, I'll put her on.' Bella held out the slimline phone. There was no way Marina could avoid it.

'Hello?' She half turned away, to stare out of the door.

'Marina.' His voice was deep and smooth. Inevitably, stupidly, a thrill of excitement skittered across her skin and she shivered. 'How's the shopping? Has Bella finally convinced you to spend my money?'

Marina darted a look at her companion, but Bella had moved away, talking to the sales assistant as she boxed the shoes. Just how much had she told him about Marina's reluctance to use his platinum credit card?

'It's going fine, thanks. It's impossible to shop with Bella and *not* spend a small fortune.'

'I'm sure it will be worth every penny.' His voice lowered to a soft burr that made her pulse gallop. 'I'm looking forward to seeing the results.'

'Why are you calling?' She sounded brusque, but that was better than letting him hear the unevenness in her breathing.

'To invite you out. Are you up to it?'

Fleetingly she wondered if she'd ever be up to coping with Ronan Carlisle. Just the sound of his voice, low and intimate in her ear, was enough to turn her inside out.

'Of course. I'm not sick.' She paused. 'When did you have in mind?'

'Tonight.'

All the breath in Marina's lungs disappeared in a sudden whoosh of fear. Tonight! That was way too early. They'd only agreed to this crazy plan a few days ago. She still wasn't sure she could manage her part in it.

More to the point, she didn't yet know how to control her

responses to Ronan Carlisle. No man had ever affected her like this. He was even disrupting her sleep. And if she played the part of his lover she'd have to stand close to him, maybe touch him, let him touch her…

'Marina?'

'I'm still here,' she said quickly.

'I'll pick you up at seven.'

Seven. That was only a few short hours away.

'I…' she gulped. 'Sure. I'll be ready.' As ready as she'd ever be. 'Where are we going? What should I wear?' This was the beginning of their masquerade, and she was determined to do the best she could.

'A cocktail party first. Then a quiet dinner. We'll go somewhere we'll be seen, but where we can talk privately. Discuss it with Bella; she'll help you choose something suitable.'

There was the sound of voices in the background, then he said, 'I've got to go. I'll see you at seven.'

And then there was silence.

Marina closed the phone carefully. Her palms were damp as she rubbed them over the cotton of her sundress. Her pulse still raced, and there was an edgy, swirling sensation in the pit of her stomach.

Three hours to transform herself. Just three hours until she had to play the part of Ronan Carlisle's mistress. She'd have to persuade a bunch of critical strangers that she was the sort of sexy female who'd catch Ronan Carlisle's interest. *And* she had to ensure Ronan had no inkling of the devastating effect he had on her.

She had to convince both herself and him that her reaction to his kiss had been an aberration, a one-off event. That he could look at her with that intense flare in his eyes, share a whispered conversation, even perhaps hold her close, and she would feel nothing.

She shivered.

Would she have the nerve to go through with it?

In the end Marina had more time than she wanted to prepare. Too much time to think and worry. She showered and carefully put on her make-up, following the instructions they'd given her at the salon. And all the time she tried to ignore the deep-seated fear that she was about to make a complete spectacle of herself.

But then how much worse could things get? No business and probably no job soon, if Charles Wakefield brought in his own staff. And Seb and Emma with a baby on the way.

Which meant she *had* to co-operate with Ronan Carlisle. If there was any chance, no matter how small, that he could get back for them what they'd lost, then she had to take it. Her personal discomfort didn't matter.

For a moment another fear edged into her thoughts. The idea that Ronan might want her to do more than put on a public show as his mistress. Was it possible he'd expect her to be so grateful for his help that she'd play the part of his lover in private too?

Her breath clogged as she froze, transfixed by the possibility.

Then common sense reasserted itself. She was letting her imagination run away with her. He'd kissed her, but only after she'd made it shamingly clear how much she craved his touch. He'd been curious. But he didn't want her. He just saw her as a tool in his scheme.

She had nothing to worry about on that score.

Marina zipped up the new dress and walked over to the mirror. There she stopped and stared, eyes wide with disbelief. The outfit looked even better now than it had in the changing room.

It had been over a year since she'd bought new clothes, and since then she'd dropped a dress size. She was slimmer. But it wasn't only that.

Her hands spread over the silky fabric that skimmed her curves so lovingly. It was unbelievable. She turned, trying to discover just what made the dress so different. So intriguing, so sinful.

It wasn't too tight, but it clung in all the right places. Places that now seemed just right. Curvaceous, not bulging. The neckline wasn't especially low—only a shadow of cleavage showed at the deeply cut square neck. She frowned, unable to put her finger on what made the dress so special.

And turned her into a different woman.

Then, suddenly, there was no time left to wonder. The doorbell pealed and she grabbed her purse. She wouldn't allow herself time for doubts now. It was too late.

But her hand shook as she reached for the front door.

Ronan stood back as the door swung open. Anticipation fizzed through his bloodstream. He hadn't seen her in days. He'd forced himself to keep away, working with renewed vigour on his commercial plans. But it had been harder than he'd expected to maintain his distance. Far too hard. For it wasn't business that had been paramount on his mind. Marina had eclipsed all else since the moment he'd seen her, vibrant and determined, at Wakefield's party.

And suddenly there she was. Marina Lucchesi, ready to play the part of his lover. She stared up at him with liquid-dark questioning eyes.

He should say something to break the thick tension in the air. But he couldn't. He stood, absorbing the body-blow to his solar plexus that had robbed him of oxygen.

By God, she was gorgeous. Arresting, with her sculpted face and hourglass figure. Why she'd hidden herself under those frumpish clothes was a mystery.

He'd imagined her like this during each restless, frustrated night. Her hair was seduction itself, a silken invitation to touch that made him clench his fists so he wouldn't reach out and grab. Her lips were a glossy dark pout that promised all the passion a man could want. Her body was a siren's: the sort a man would dream about for the rest of his life.

The telltale tightening across his belly and thighs was testament to the power of her.

'You look lovely, Marina.' He watched confusion and delight flare in her eyes, and wondered at her reaction to the simple compliment. She obviously wasn't used to praise.

'Is it okay for the party?' She gestured to the dress, as if unsure.

'Perfect,' he assured her. 'You'll be the sexiest woman there.'

Her eyes widened at his words, and her full lips parted just a fraction.

It was pure invitation. Impossible to ignore.

He stepped close, bending his head before she could protest or move away. But he dredged up a sliver of restraint at the last moment and pressed his lips to her brow, not her luscious mouth. He'd discovered how dangerous her kisses were, and he was determined not to be sidetracked again. For the moment at least.

He inhaled her delicate scent, trailing his mouth for one exquisite moment over her whisper-soft hair, feeling her intimate warmth against him.

He couldn't repress the tremor of raw desire that racked his rigid muscles. She was pure, feminine invitation. He breathed deep and forced himself to move away.

She wore black, a shimmering dress sprinkled with silvery starbursts, that clung to her like a lover's hands. On her feet were the sexiest shoes he'd ever seen. And those legs…

Hell! Tonight would be the ultimate test of his control. He'd much rather lead her to her bedroom, strip the clothes from her and lose himself in her body.

But he knew how stubborn she was. Had seen the obstinate tilt of her chin when she'd argued against his plans. He remembered her sudden reserve, how she'd pushed him away. Despite her body's undeniable weakness for his caresses, her mind was set against any further intimacies.

This wasn't the time. Not yet. Somehow he'd have to find a way to ignore the primitive instinct to reach out and simply take her.

Tonight was the night he introduced Marina to the world as his lover. A ploy to lure Wakefield, yes. But, more importantly, a means of keeping Marina exactly where he wanted her.

And he was a man used to getting exactly what he wanted. Every time.

CHAPTER EIGHT

MARINA sank back into the embrace of the leather seat and tried to slow her beating heart as the sports car cruised the city streets.

From the moment she'd opened the door to Ronan Carlisle it was as if she'd stepped out of her mundane world and into a fairytale.

No fantasy prince had ever looked more handsome or more potently male. The sight of him had set off a deep-seated fire of need and a ridiculous longing that had robbed her of words. She hadn't been able to read his expression. But there'd been a tension about him, as if he was poised on the brink of decisive action, that had held her in thrall with its intensity. Then he'd stepped close, and the world had tilted on its axis.

Marina's eyes fluttered shut as scorching desire rose at the memory.

She'd almost expected him to sweep her into his arms and kiss her like he had before, till reason disintegrated in an explosion of new sensations. She'd *wanted* him to.

But of course he hadn't. The other night had been a mistake. He probably regretted it as much as she should—*did*.

Instead it had been a chaste kiss, a gentle salutation that a brother might give. A little much-needed encouragement. That's all.

Yet, no matter how firmly she told herself that, her reaction was the same. An urgent craving—not only for his approval, but his passion. Her whole body had come alive, awareness had ignited as he'd stepped close. Her senses had clamoured for more, more, more.

How stupid was that? She was on fire for a man who viewed her simply as an asset in a business manoeuvre.

She had to cling to that knowledge and keep her feet firmly on the ground. She was no match for his sophistication, could never compete with the type of woman he *really* wanted. She had to remember what this was all about.

She opened her eyes and slid a sideways glance at him. Even with his jaw clamped hard and his brow furrowed, he was the handsomest man she'd ever seen. He looked almost grim, and Marina wondered if he too was having second thoughts about his scheme.

'Tell me if you tire,' he said abruptly. 'We'll only stay at the party long enough to make an impression.'

'I'll be fine,' she murmured, wondering just how big a lie that was. She wasn't worried she'd collapse—her difficulty the night she'd confronted Wakefield had been due as much to stress as physical weakness. And now, after just a few days, she was feeling much stronger.

But would she be able to carry off this masquerade? Despite the new clothes, she couldn't imagine anyone believing she'd captured Ronan Carlisle's attention. He could have any sultry, gorgeous beauty he wanted.

And would she be able to hold her own tonight among Sydney's elite? She was a homebody. An ordinary office worker. She had no practice at rubbing shoulders with the rich and famous.

She turned her head to stare out of the side window. For one unguarded moment she allowed herself to admit the devastating truth. Parading herself as a *femme fatale* was preposterous. She was sure to be found out.

But that was the risk she had to take. If there was a slim chance of setting things right for Seb and Emma and the baby, then she'd do it gladly.

But her secret fear was much worse. That by playing this charade of intimacy with Ronan Carlisle, he might discover how she felt about him. Learn how devastating he was to her peace of mind and her willpower.

That secretly, in some hidden inner chamber of her heart, she wished it was true: that she and Ronan really were lovers.

An hour later, Marina was stunned at how easily she'd slipped into this role of Ronan's devising. No one had shown by word or look that they thought it odd, her being with the most powerful, most drop-dead gorgeous man at the crowded party. Maybe they were all too polite to hint at what they really thought—that she didn't belong.

All she'd had to do was stand close and look as if she had eyes for no one but him.

No acting required!

Awareness vibrated through her every time Ronan moved or gestured at her side. It was frightening how attuned to him she was, even now, when his attention was on the man who'd come up to discuss business trends. She remembered him from Wakefield's reception of course, where he'd waylaid them on their way out. But it was only now she recognised him. After all, it wasn't every day you bumped into a senior government minister in the flesh.

Ronan turned and caught her gaze. A shaft of heat seared her. Shaken, she dropped her eyes and bent her head to sip champagne.

The men finished their discussion. The politician excused himself for interrupting them. She smiled and shook his hand, then watched him turn away.

But her smile died as, through the shifting colours of the crowded room, she saw a face she knew. A pair of eyes fixed on her, absorbed. She swallowed hard and froze.

Charles Wakefield.

Her illusion of confidence shattered in an instant.

How would he react to her presence? Would he embarrass her in front of everyone? Or would he ignore her?

'Marina, look at me.' Ronan's voice was low and compelling.

She turned. 'Did you see him? Wakefield—'

'I know.' He moved in front of her to eclipse the room so she could see no one else. She tilted her head and looked up into his mesmerising eyes. 'There's no need to be nervous,' he said. 'Wakefield's not going to make a scene. Not with me here to stop him.'

Marina wished she could absorb the confidence that radiated from the big man in front of her. Dread carved a hollow sensation in the pit of her stomach. A few days ago she'd wanted nothing more than a meeting with Wakefield. Now the very idea of it made her feel sick.

Ronan took the glass from her trembling hold and placed it on a nearby table.

'Touch me.' His lips moved bare inches from her face.

She couldn't have heard him right. 'Sorry?'

'Touch me, Marina. Now, while he's looking at us.' His eyes blazed with an inner fire and the curve of his lips as he smiled down at her was a sensual promise.

She swallowed, stunned at how realistic that lover's smile of his looked. Scared by the inevitable reaction it stirred low in her body.

Tentatively she raised her hand, closed her fingers round the soft weave of linen on his arm. The muscle beneath shifted and bunched. She felt the gentle exhalation of his breath on her upturned face. Without thinking she leaned in to him, drawn to his heat and to the subtle male scent that had teased her senses all evening.

'That's it,' he encouraged. 'Perfect.'

For a heartbeat they stared at each other. Then he wrapped an arm round her, drawing her close so his heat seared her right through the thin fabric of her dress. Her breath stopped in her throat at the forbidden images that simple contact evoked.

Ronan turned her towards the full-length windows that opened onto the roof garden. They stepped into the warm, scented evening, not pausing till they reached the shelter of a secluded loggia. His fingers splayed across her hip in what must look like a mark of ownership. To her it felt like a brand, pure fire that sizzled across her skin and deep into her soul, marking her very being.

Nonsense! She was letting her imagination run away with her. This was all make-believe.

Here in the shadow of overhanging jasmine they were virtually invisible from inside. But Wakefield must have seen them leave. Was he curious enough to follow them outside?

Ronan obviously thought so. He stayed close enough to look like a lover.

And that was what she had to remember. It was an act. She had to concentrate on playing her part.

She drew a deep breath, heady with the perfume of flowers, and stared out over the spectacular cityscape, fighting to block out all sensation and concentrate on the view. The harbour below them glowed like shot silk with the last reflection of the dying sun. Around it a multitude of lights from the surrounding city had sprung to life like sparkling gems.

'Beautiful.' Ronan's deep voice was like the brush of rich silk across her skin. She looked up and found him watching her, intent. Her stomach plunged in a bottomless dive as excitement sped up her pulse another notch. The shadows of an overhead vine cast his features in shade, but she could make out the strong lines of his throat and jaw, the glitter of his eyes as he looked down at her.

Whatever she'd been about to say died. The passion in his voice, the tension vibrating from his body, seemed so real.

A game, Marina. Remember it's a game.

But despite that knowledge, despite the last vestiges of common sense, she responded, swaying closer, forgetting her vow to be strong.

In the distance a melody sounded, a shout of laughter. But here there was only the sound of her heartbeat, drumming like a hammer. Her breath, raw and shallow in her throat.

What would it be like if Ronan Carlisle, so virile, so tempting, were to look at her with real desire? Not as a ploy to convince Wakefield. Not because he felt sorry for her, as he had the other night.

Her mind skittered away from the dangerous idea.

'Is he watching?' she asked, hoping Ronan would mistake her breathlessness for a whisper.

He didn't respond, just wrapped his other arm around her and pulled her close, so that the heat of him enveloped her. His elusive male scent invaded her senses, potent and musky, like a taste of velvet against her lips.

Something inside her flared into life, shimmering and exciting. Expectation.

Staring into his eyes, she wondered frantically how she'd got herself into this. She was playing a part, but she was way out of her depth. This man who was supposed to be her ally had suddenly become a threat.

Ronan Carlisle was far more dangerous, she now realised, than Wakefield, the man who'd stolen her birthright. More dangerous than any mere business competitor or swindling cheat could ever be.

Ronan was out of her league, a master player in a complex game where she was just a pawn.

He made her feel like she'd never felt before. Like a woman, vibrant and passionate. Wanting.

Wanting what she couldn't have. What she shouldn't want from him.

She opened her mouth to speak. To break the spell of the seductive setting and her own fantasies. Of the passion Ronan projected for the benefit of the man she guessed watched them from the shadows.

But it was too late.

Arms as unyielding as steel drew her up to a body that was all hard muscle and bone and flaring heat. His head lowered, lips warm and sure against hers.

And Marina melted into his embrace, promising herself that she would give herself up to these glorious sensations once. Just one last time, to convince Wakefield. And then she'd step away.

Ronan's mouth was surprisingly soft, coaxing her to kiss him back. There was none of the ravaging energy she'd experienced before. Yet this kiss was just as stunning, destroying all thought, inviting complete capitulation.

He lifted a hand to her hair, cupping her head as he sought better access to her lips.

He tasted like sparkling wine and pure, intoxicating man. Like all the sins of temptation put together. And she couldn't get enough of him. She wanted to burrow closer to his warmth, to the easy caress of his mouth, to the exciting hardness of his big frame.

The sensations exploding through her were like firebursts. They flared and spread, searing every nerve with a need she fought desperately to resist.

But the desires he awakened were too compelling to deny.

She lifted her hands, sliding them up against his shirt to rest against the heat of his chest. His heartbeat thudded beneath her palm, strong and steady, and her head swam at the intimacy.

It wasn't enough. Involuntarily she squirmed against him, fighting her own weakness. But common sense had deserted her. Instead she gave in to the primitive need that pounded in her blood, slipping her hands down so she could wrap her arms round him, beneath his jacket. Holding him tight, as if he were hers.

He stepped closer, his thighs settling on either side of hers so she was cradled in his intimate heat. His other arm lashed tight round her waist, making breathing difficult.

But she barely noticed. For his tongue slid along her lips, inviting her to open for him. And of course she did, responding mindlessly to the sensuous promise of his expertise.

Heat. Velvety darkness. Mingled breaths. The delicious rasp of tongue against tongue. A shared erotic awareness that scorched all rational thought from her brain. And, above all, the rising need for more.

She clutched at him, dimly aware of being bowed back over Ronan's arm by the power of his embrace. He was closer than ever, pushing against her breasts, her hips, her thighs. Comprehensively claiming her mouth.

His arm moved from her waist, slipping down over her hip, and then lower still. His long fingers splayed over her bottom, pulling her higher and tighter against his hard body. It was a movement so explicit that she gasped.

Not with surprise or outrage.

With the realisation that she wanted still more.

She wanted everything she'd dreamed of from a lover. All the heat and passion. All the love. Everything she'd never had.

And she wanted it from Ronan.

For an instant the illusion held. Then his mouth relinquished hers and she gulped in a shuddering breath. He straightened, pulling her up with him, but he stepped back a tiny pace too. Enough to keep the illusion of intimacy, but, she realised achingly as her body throbbed with unfulfilled desire, not close enough.

Flame scorched her cheeks. It was only the strength of his hands that kept her upright. Her legs trembled with a weakness that had nothing to do with her injuries.

He didn't speak, but she saw the way his chest heaved. Lack of oxygen. She'd clung to him like a limpet. It was a wonder he'd been able to breathe at all.

It was a miracle she hadn't climbed up his big body in her desperate passion.

And all he'd done was kiss her.

Hell!

She squeezed her eyes shut, knowing she couldn't have been more embarrassingly transparent if she'd tried.

So much for being wary. For doubting his plan. For being a self-sufficient, independent woman. For telling herself she could control her reaction to him.

Nothing had mattered except the craving his touch had evoked. Not her self-respect, nor their situation, nor the knowledge that to him she was no more than a temporary business partner.

'Marina.' His husky whisper set need spiralling anew in her abdomen. She opened her eyes and looked at his shirt, not ready to lift her chin and meet his probing gaze.

One of his buttons had slipped undone. Had she done that? Horrified, she kept her gaze fixed on it, wishing she had the nerve to reach casually across and do it up.

But that would mean touching him again.

Yes! screamed the savage woman he'd awakened.

Absolutely not, dictated the grim voice of self-preservation.

How had she succumbed yet again to this man? He'd only had to touch her and her defences had melted to nothing.

'Marina,' Ronan said again. 'We've got company.'

Even as he spoke she heard the voices coming nearer. Just as well they'd stopped when they had.

She darted a look up at him and, sure enough, he watched her intently. His face was expressionless, but the throb of his pulse at the base of his neck testified to the urgency of their embrace.

Marina pushed back her shoulders and tilted her chin. But she wouldn't look him in the eye again. Instead she swung round towards the approaching couple. They paused beside a huge potted tree strung with lights. No mistaking that profile, she realised as she recognised one of the pair. Charles Wakefield.

She waited for the dread to engulf her. The trepidation. But this time it didn't come. Instead all her senses were alert, trying to read the body language of the man beside her.

Ronan Carlisle must have been born a natural poker player. Not by so much as a movement did he betray his thoughts or feelings.

'So, it looks like the mountain is coming to Mohammed. I knew his curiosity would get the better of him.' Ronan leaned close to whisper the words against her ear, and it took all her control not to shiver at the delicious sensation of his hot breath against her skin.

'Are you ready, Marina?'

'Of course.'

'Marina?' His hand lifted her chin, forcing her to look at him. The touch of his hard fingers against her flesh sent another riot of sensation through her and she set her jaw, desperately searching for her shattered defences.

His expression was quizzical. 'Just remember, you're besotted with me. Don't worry about Wakefield or anything else. Okay?'

'Okay.'

Nothing could be easier, she decided glumly, as he draped his arm round her shoulders and pulled her in close against his side, so they looked like lovers. Even that casual embrace made her heart thud out of control.

She wouldn't even have to act. She had a sinking feeling that *besotted* described her feelings all too accurately.

A cynical voice in her brain told her it was simply to be expected. Ronan was gorgeous, powerful, sexy, rich, and he had a take-charge attitude that appealed to her despite her own need to assert herself. The fact that he kissed like every woman's erotic fantasy had nothing whatever to do with this appalling weakness.

'Chin up, Princess,' he said. 'Just remember what we agreed and it'll be fine.'

What they'd agreed. Right. Marina ticked off the points in her mind.

One: she was to focus on Ronan. She could check that one off.

Two: as far as Wakefield was concerned, Ronan was looking after her now. She'd be angry with Wakefield, but she'd appear to have other things on her mind. Double check.

'Oops, sorry. I didn't see you guys.' A giggling voice interrupted her thoughts, and she turned to see a blonde who looked all of seventeen on Wakefield's arm.

Righteous anger surged through her. Not only a thief and a cheat. A cradle-snatcher as well.

The kid was unsteady on her feet, and Marina wondered if it was due to the teetering heels she wore or the oversized cocktail glass she waved in one hand.

Marina frowned, and immediately Ronan's arm slipped down to tighten round her waist, snatching her breath away as she experienced again that incredible melting sensation deep in her body.

'Charles.' It was Ronan who spoke.

'Carlisle. Loitering in the dark?' Wakefield's smug tone set Marina's teeth on edge. Despite Ronan's embrace, she had to fight the urge to spit venom at the man who'd cheated her brother.

Wakefield turned to face her, the curiosity obvious in his expression. He eyed her up and down so thoroughly she felt queasy. Her dress was designed to catch a man's attention, but this was one man whose regard made her feel as if she needed a wash.

'And Ms Lucchesi. I must say I didn't expect to see you here.'

Marina stared back at him, wondering what sort of guy could threaten her with a lawsuit for slander, plan to throw her out of his reception, and now act as if she were an interesting specimen for study.

An arrogant son of a bitch who believed he had to answer to no one, she decided.

'I could say the same,' she retorted. 'If I'd known you'd be here I wouldn't have come.'

'Now, Ms Lucchesi. Marina.' He spread his hands in a show of openness. 'No need for that, surely? Our conversation the other day wasn't helpful, but it was hardly the most appropriate time or place.'

His patronising tone made the hairs on her neck prickle, and

Marina was grateful for the reassuring sweep of Ronan's hand against her waist as he held her against him. She looked up to see him watching her, his gaze giving nothing away. It was good to have an ally. Even one who made her feel far too much.

'I see you have someone else to speak for you now. How very convenient.' No mistaking the sarcasm in Wakefield's tone.

Ronan's baritone cut across him. 'My relationship with Marina is private, Charles, but I can tell you this: *convenient* isn't how I'd describe it.'

'Hardly,' added Marina, fixing Wakefield with a glare that should have burnt the smarmy grin right off his face. 'Nor is it any of your business. But I speak for myself and always will,' she added in freezing accents.

The girl with Wakefield looked uncertainly from one to the other, clearly wondering what she'd walked into. But Wakefield's expression was intent. Marina could almost hear the wheels turning over as he sifted their words, read their body language.

Could he really be putting two and two together and coming up with five?

'My mistake,' he said smoothly. He looked at Ronan, then back to her again, and Marina held her breath, wondering what was coming next. Had he already decided this was a far-fetched plot? She'd known no one would believe they were an item.

'We still have unfinished business, Marina,' Wakefield continued in a suave tone. 'Our last discussion didn't resolve anything, and, on reflection, I feel I owe you an explanation of what took place between your brother and me.'

Marina bit her tongue rather than blurt out that she knew exactly what had occurred. Seb had told her.

Wakefield took her silence for agreement. 'We should meet.' He paused, bestowing his toothy smile. 'And we can discuss the situation.'

Stunned, she nodded. Surely it couldn't be so easy? Could it? Was he really promising her a chance to negotiate?

'That's exactly what I'd like.' She had to remind herself that it was easy to arrange a meeting. That didn't mean Wakefield had any intention of making redress.

'Good,' he said, and his smile widened disconcertingly, reminding her again of a hungry carnivore. 'Give me your number, and I'll get my PA to organise it.'

She'd opened her mouth to respond when Ronan spoke. 'Good idea, Charles. Just have him call my home to arrange a time.'

She gaped as he continued blithely, 'Marina's moving in with me.'

CHAPTER NINE

A FEW minutes later Ronan watched Marina steer the younger woman across the roof garden and into the penthouse. The girl looked green around the gills, and Marina had decided they both needed to freshen their make-up.

He suppressed a smile, wondering if she'd use the privacy to give vent to feelings she'd been unable to acknowledge in front of Wakefield.

When he'd dropped the news that they'd be living together she'd stiffened in shock, her whole body taut as a bowstring. He knew what it had cost her not to ask what the hell he was up to. He'd felt the anger well inside her, a palpable force. But she'd restricted herself to a burning stare which might have been mistaken in the shadows for passionate.

Wakefield had been ogling her like a kid staring in a candy shop window. But that bombshell had made him jerk back in disbelief, then shoot an assessing glance between the two of them. Obviously he'd made it his business to know Ronan never invited lovers to share his home.

But instead of it warning Wakefield off, he was still sniffing around Marina. The 'private property' signs Ronan had posted didn't deter him.

Just as he'd expected. Wakefield found her attractive in her ultra-feminine clothes and make-up. Any man would.

The news that she belonged to Ronan, and apparently meant significantly more to him than any previous lover, had sent the man into a frenzy of curiosity.

But Wakefield felt much more than curiosity. There was no mistaking the leer on his face as he watched Marina support the other girl through the door of the apartment.

That look told Ronan all he needed to know. Wakefield would take the bait and chase her, as much for her own sake as for the opportunity of besting his rival. All he had to do was play Wakefield a little longer, choose his moment, and then reel him in.

Ronan waited for the surge of elation. Of satisfaction.

And waited.

Why wasn't he pleased at how easy this would be? He took a moment to assess the emotion gripping him so rigidly round the shoulders.

It was sheer bloody anger. Fury that a low-life like Wakefield thought he stood a chance with someone as intelligent and classy as Marina.

Marina was *his*! His alone.

His pulse quickened at the thought of how much he'd enjoy wiping that leer off Wakefield's face.

'I have to hand it to you, Carlisle, you're a quick worker.' Wakefield took a swig of what smelt like pure Scotch and grinned at him. 'It's less than a week since she gatecrashed my reception, and I'd bet you hadn't even met her before that.' His eyes narrowed. 'Or was it you who put her up to that little stunt?'

Ronan settled his shoulder against a pillar and crossed one leg over the other, projecting nonchalance. It was a child's ploy, but he knew how much Wakefield would hate it.

'Sorry to disappoint you, Charles, but I had no idea Marina was going to be there. You know I've always left the Machiavellian stuff to you.'

But things have just changed.

And he was going to get a hell of a lot of satisfaction from making Wakefield pay for the damage he'd inflicted. And for daring to leer at Marina.

'I'd never seen or heard of Marina before that night,' Ronan added.

Wakefield flicked a glance in the direction of the penthouse.

'And obviously you took her home afterwards.' Ronan caught an undercurrent of pique.

He nodded. 'That's right.'

'Well, well.' Wakefield spread his lips in a lascivious smirk. 'She must really be something in the sack if she's hooked you in less than a week. What's her secret? Does she play the innocent or the tart?'

The impulse to grab the slimy bastard by the neck and crush the air from his windpipe was almost overpowering. Ronan's hands flexed convulsively and he straightened to loom over him. There was a savage satisfaction in seeing the immediate flare of terror in Wakefield's eyes. Ronan had to fight the temptation to deck the little weasel, since he couldn't throttle him.

Years of ignoring his petty games had taught Ronan control in the face of provocation. He'd even reined in his thirst for blood when he'd learned what Wakefield had done to Cleo. It had been almost impossible, but that was the only way to protect her. If Wakefield learned the truth about her recent 'illness' he'd make it public knowledge in the blink of an eye.

But now Wakefield had gone too far. The surge of primitive emotions was too strong for Ronan to contain. And that was a warning sign in itself.

'Don't go there,' Ronan growled, in a voice that was pure intimidation. He took a single pace forward and saw Wakefield shrink back.

He got the message all right. It was clear in the whites of his eyes and his defensive posture. But Ronan wasn't taking chances.

'Just one word like that to Marina, or about her, and you'll wish you'd never been born. Have you got that?'

'Sure, sure.' Wakefield took another step away. 'No need for threats. Obviously I got the wrong idea. I didn't realise you were serious about the girl.' His gaze, intent and assessing, swept Ronan.

'Your mistake. Just don't make it again.'

And so the trap closed, with an echoing clang.

This time Ronan recognised the sizzle of anticipation as he saw his plan swing into action. Wakefield wanted what Ronan had: Marina. His ego was so colossal he actually thought he could entice her away with his brittle charm and empty promises.

Wakefield waved his drink in the direction of the party. 'Here she comes now.'

Ronan turned to see the two girls heading towards them. His mouth dried at the silhouette of Marina's figure, backlit by the lights of the apartment. The enticing sway of her hips as she walked towards him matched the urgent tattoo of his pulse. Blood drummed through his body as he remembered the feel of her luscious curves pulled up hard against him. Of her hands, tentative but seductive, stoking his need wherever they touched.

'I have to admit, Carlisle, you can pick them. She really is something.'

Wakefield was trying to lighten the atmosphere. But the sense of primal ownership Ronan felt as he watched her made him want to whisk her away somewhere private. Somewhere secluded from every other man. He didn't want Wakefield looking at her. Not when he knew what was going on in that gutter that passed for his mind.

'If she'd dressed like that when she came to see me I might have taken her more seriously,' Wakefield muttered.

Which just confirmed what Ronan had always known—Wakefield was as shallow as they came. It was surface glitter that caught his eye. Hadn't the guy seen beyond Marina's god-awful suit and scraped-back hair that first night?

Ronan shook his head in disbelief, remembering her spirit and intelligence, her determination, her sheer bravery that night as she'd fought a losing battle and ignored the odds. The way passion had lit her from within, the fire in her eyes and the classic sculpted lines of her face. All had accentuated her vibrant beauty.

Wakefield was worse than a conniving bastard.

He was a fool.

* * *

Ronan must take her for a fool, Marina decided half an hour later. Avoiding his probing gaze, she looked around the exclusive restaurant. After the dizzying flash of lights from the paparazzi as they entered, the dining room was quiet, elegantly opulent and very discreet.

She didn't understand what Ronan was up to. That lie about moving in with him had been totally unnecessary. Yet it seemed he expected her to accept it without argument. Why should she move into his home? Surely they didn't need to go so far to convince Wakefield they were lovers?

And after tonight she was even less certain she had the stamina to play the part of Ronan's mistress.

When she'd returned to the roof garden to see both men watching her, she'd wanted to turn tail and run. Wakefield's sly looks had made her want to hide. And Ronan's steady, impenetrable gaze had heated her body to tingling, sensuous excitement.

He scared her witless.

A single touch of his hand sent her nervous system into overload. If she had to pretend to intimacy with him for an extended period he was sure to discover she wasn't acting. That her desire for him was shamingly real.

She was in lust with Ronan Carlisle.

He'd only have to crook his finger and she'd have the fight of her life trying to keep her sanity long enough to resist him. Even worse, the way he made her feel—as if she were precious, protected and cared for—appealed far too much. If she weren't careful her emotions would override her common sense.

And that would be disastrous. He would never want a woman like her.

'All right.' Ronan's low murmur sent a shiver of delicious awareness through her. 'The waiter's gone, so you can say it. No one will hear but me.'

She lifted her gaze. He leaned back in his chair on the other side of the small table, the epitome of arrogant assurance. His eyes glittered in the subtle candlelight and his smile would melt the hardest female heart.

Pure sex on legs. That was what he was.

Too much man for you, Marina.

'I've changed my mind,' she said flatly. 'I want out of this charade.'

She read a flicker of emotion in his face but couldn't pin it down.

'I didn't have you pegged as a quitter, Marina. Or are you just frightened?'

'What would I be frightened of?'

He shrugged. 'You tell me. I don't pretend to know what goes on in your mind.'

'I'm not scared,' she said, lifting her chin and looking him in the eye so he wouldn't guess how big a lie that was. She felt colour wash across her throat and cheeks as he surveyed her but she refused to look away.

'If it's not fear, why give up so easily?'

She shrugged. 'This isn't going to work. I never really believed it would, but I was desperate enough to think we might make Wakefield change his mind.'

'And you're not desperate now?'

Her breath caught. Trust him to remind her of her obligations. Of course she was desperate.

'That's not the point,' she answered. 'I can't make Wakefield give back what he's stolen just because he thinks I'm your…'

'*Lover* is the word you're looking for.'

Marina watched his mouth shape the word, and something short-circuited in her brain. All she could think of was the feel of those lips against hers, the intimate caress of his tongue, the way his hands had splayed so possessively, so knowingly, over her body.

And of how she'd all but begged him for more. Not once, but twice. And the second time, on the roof terrace, not even the fact that they were being watched had stopped her.

She reached for her water and drank half of it.

'You may not be able to make Wakefield surrender it, but I can.' From anyone else the words would have sounded glib. But not from him.

She read the grim implacability in his face and knew a fleeting twinge of sympathy for Charles Wakefield. He should never have messed with Ronan. Marina couldn't conceive of anyone besting Ronan in this mood. His angular jaw looked dangerous and his eyes shone bright with purpose. A man who played for keeps.

'I know what I'm doing, Marina. I have every intention of succeeding.'

She believed him. As far as his pursuit of Wakefield went.

But further than that she couldn't trust him. Not when he held all the cards and used her to suit his own ends. He might need her now, but she was part of a bigger scheme that he alone understood. That made her vulnerable.

And something about his plan didn't sit right. Instinct told her it wasn't what it seemed. That there was more to it than Ronan had told her.

Worse still, she knew that against Ronan Carlisle she didn't have enough defences. Her sixth sense screamed at her to get away while she still could.

'You'd be unwise to back out now.'

'Why? What do you know that I don't?' She leaned forward and caught of glint of satisfaction in Ronan's eyes as he crossed his arms. The action drew her attention to his shoulders, wide and powerful beneath his jacket.

'You didn't see the way he looked at you?'

'He made my skin crawl, if that's what you mean. But that doesn't prove anything.' If the situation weren't so ridiculous it would be pathetic. The night she finally looked half convincing as a desirable woman and it had to be for a toad like Wakefield!

'He's definitely interested. He swallowed the bait.'

'How can you be sure?'

'Let's just say he made himself obvious when you weren't around.'

Marina registered Ronan's disapproving tone and decided she didn't want to know what Wakefield had said.

'So he's interested. So what? There are lots of women in Sydney, and I'm sure he spreads himself pretty wide.'

'The difference is your connection with me. I made it clear you were someone special. I posted "no trespassing" signs even he couldn't miss.'

Despite her resolve, Marina was intrigued. More than intrigued. Delighted. Some idiotic, credulous part of her wanted to pretend Ronan had done that for real, because he cared for her. How pathetic was that?

'You did?'

'I did.' His expression held her spellbound, sucked the air from her lungs. 'Why do you think I told him you were moving in with me?'

'That's what I've been wondering.'

His lips twisted in wry amusement. 'Wakefield knows I've never invited a woman to share my home.'

Marina reached for her glass again and drained it. Anything to counter the fatuous smile that threatened to spread across her face.

He was playing a part. He didn't really want her living with him. But illogically she was pleased none of his previous lovers had shared his house.

Even though she was a lover in name only.

'The guy's hooked.' He interrupted her train of thought. 'One good look at you and he wasn't thinking with his brain. And when I threatened him—'

'You did *what?*'

'I warned him off my territory.' He shrugged those massive shoulders. As if Wakefield was merely a nuisance, not a danger.

For a bedazzled instant, for more, Marina wondered what it would be like to let this dominant, powerful man share her burdens. Solve her problems. Protect her. Let her relinquish the weight of responsibilities she'd accepted at thirteen.

As if.

Anyway, it would probably drive her crazy.

'When Wakefield learned I was serious about you he could barely contain his excitement. He's decided you're my weak spot, and he can't wait to try luring you away. Especially now he holds a trump card.'

'Sorry?'

'Your business, Marina. He'll use it as a bargaining chip.'

As if she could be bought for the price of the company. Or, she realised, a bitter taste in her mouth, just for the promise to discuss it. Wakefield would never relinquish it.

Which meant she had no choice but to go along with Ronan's scheme.

She felt trapped, as if the walls had closed in on her. All avenues were barred except the one he held open. She couldn't turn away.

There was Seb and Emma. And the baby. Seb could find another job, start from scratch. But he'd struggle for years because of a single stupid mistake.

And it was her family business. She couldn't let it go so easily. Not to a shark like Wakefield. He'd strip its assets and move on, leaving their employees out of work. People who'd been with them for years: loyal, hardworking, many of them too old to find another job easily, despite their experience.

They were all links in the heavy, inescapable chain that bound her to Ronan Carlisle.

Marina stared at him. The subdued lighting couldn't conceal the hard decisiveness of his angular jaw, the powerful set of his shoulders as he leaned back at ease in his chair. His face was unrevealing, but even in repose it spoke of strength and determination. He was a man who played to win. A man who could get her what she needed.

As long as she survived the experience.

'But if he thinks I've moved in with you he won't make a move.'

Ronan shook his head. 'He'll see you as a greater challenge. He has an ego the size of Antarctica. He won't consider the possibility that he can't get you.'

His lips turned up in a taut smile that made her shiver. 'He won't be able to resist, now he believes you're my woman.'

The shiver turned into a thrill of forbidden excitement at his words.

She was being ridiculous, but she couldn't help it. Not when the touch of his eyes was a hot caress across her bare skin. His elusive scent, dark and masculine and provocative, drew her heightened senses to fever-pitch.

Ronan's deep blue gaze pinned her. 'Whenever he sees us together he'll be convinced I'm serious about you.'

Marina gulped. The fire in his eyes made her skin sizzle. How would she cope playing up close and personal with him for Wakefield's benefit?

'But I don't have to move in,' she countered.

He raised one eyebrow in disbelief. 'Of course you do. Everything has to be as it seems. Wakefield may be an egotistical bastard but he's cunning. That's what makes him so dangerous.'

Marina sagged back in her chair, suddenly exhausted as the inexorable net closed round her again. She'd committed herself to this dangerous game. She had no choice, other than defeat. And she refused to give in.

But a dark fear welled deep inside her. She was way out of her depth. No longer in control.

She stared at the man who'd taken over her life. Could she really trust him to succeed, to deliver what he promised? Could she trust herself to play this role and no more? No stupid dreams, no pathetic hopes and longing?

'And your house is for sale,' he added. 'You'll be moving soon anyway.'

'It's been sold,' she blurted out. Seb had been waiting with the news when she arrived home today. He'd been a picture of guilt, knowing it was his folly that had driven her out of the house their father had built.

Ronan raised one dark eyebrow. 'So soon?'

She nodded, not trusting herself to elaborate. Of course it was just what they'd needed—the news of a buyer, and one willing to pay full price at that. And in the circumstances she'd felt unable to object to the request for an immediate settlement. She'd planned to spend tomorrow searching for a flat. No way could she take up Seb's offer of a room with him and Emma.

The sooner she moved out the better. The place was too full of memories. A lifetime of them.

She shouldn't pine for an empty house. Yet she had to swallow down the lump of grief in her throat. This loss was the final straw.

After all she'd been through she'd used up her reserves of strength, just forcing herself not to give up. Now she was too tired, too physically weak, to fight any more.

The warmth of Ronan's large hand enfolded hers, and she blinked back the film that blurred her eyes.

'In that case you can move in straight away.'

'I suppose I can.' She slumped in her seat, conscious again that she didn't have a choice.

It had been a hectic couple of days, an emotional few months. Right now she felt every minute of them weighing her down.

His thumb brushed across her wrist and her pulse jumped. 'It will be all right.' His voice was low and husky, as if he understood her despair.

She nodded. But she didn't look up at him till he lifted her hand. Her eyes widened as he lowered his head, the expression in his eyes concealed. She felt his warm breath on the back of her hand and shivered.

Then her own breath caught in her throat as he turned her hand and pressed a kiss to the centre of her palm. A tender, slow, utterly seductive kiss that ignited a roaring burst of sensations and made her arm jerk. But he held her firmly, cupping her fingers so that she in turn caressed him: his jaw, his lips.

'I promise, Marina,' he murmured, his mouth brushing her sensitive flesh with each syllable.

Shafts of fire ran along her arm and through her body, arrowing to the secret centre of her femininity. She trembled at the intensity, the sheer blatant potency of her reaction.

He curled her fingers around his and lifted his head. Then he signalled to a waiter, and moments later the sommelier appeared with a bottle of vintage champagne.

Through it all Ronan held her hand. And for the life of her Marina couldn't summon the willpower to pull away. Not when it felt so good.

The wine was poured and they were alone again. Ronan handed her a glass. His eyes were bright with an emotion she couldn't read and his body seemed to pulse with leashed energy, as if he couldn't wait to put his plan into action. Just being near that intense power was exciting.

'I'll take care of everything, Marina. Don't worry.'

He paused and raised his glass in salute. 'To success.'

Fervently Marina added her own silent toast. *To survival.*

CHAPTER TEN

'WELCOME to my home.' Ronan held out his hand to help Marina from the car. She hesitated, but he deliberately stood close, blocking her exit, so she had to accept his assistance.

'Thank you.'

He repressed a smile as she placed her hand in his. Did she experience it too, that frisson of superb sensation when they touched?

She turned her head away as she stood up, looking at the house rather than meeting his eyes.

Of course she felt it. She'd been avoiding his touch ever since they'd met. Almost jumped out of her skin whenever he allowed himself the luxury of brushing into contact with her.

The realisation tightened the coil of ever-present need deep inside him.

But once again she was shying away from him, nervous as an unbroken filly. For an otherwise confident woman, her anxiety when he got near was intriguing. And he was sure it wasn't an act.

Now he cursed himself for insisting on her new wardrobe. He'd promised himself he wouldn't rush her. Would give her time to adjust to the incandescent physical attraction between them since it so obviously unnerved her.

But hell! It was *killing* him.

He wasn't used to shy women. Usually he was kept busy fending them off. And nor was he used to waiting for something he wanted as much as he wanted Marina.

What he needed right now was to have her camouflaged

in one of her old sack dresses. Not the new Marina, with her rippling hair loose, her voluptuous curves and slim waist discreetly accentuated in trousers and a sleeveless waistcoat top.

Ronan dropped his eyes. Five buttons. He swallowed. Only five buttons between him and—

'Your house is lovely,' she said, snapping him out of his distraction.

He stepped back, allowing her space. Then he turned, put a proprietorial hand to the small of her back and drew her towards his home, the perfect host. As long as he could ignore the warmth of her body, the scent of her hair just a touch away.

It was an old house, heritage-listed. Gravel crunched underfoot as they approached the wide front doors.

'I'm glad you approve. I want you to be comfortable here, Marina.'

She darted a glance at him, filled with such a mix of emotions it was impossible to read. He knew she didn't want to be here. She'd made that abundantly clear, right up to this morning, when the removalists had stripped her home bare.

But she had no choice other than to accept his hospitality. He'd made sure of that.

'Come and meet Mrs Sinclair, my housekeeper. She's looking forward to having another woman in the house.'

The tour of the property took some time. And Marina's reactions were fascinating.

He'd been asked more than once if his home could be featured in one lifestyle magazine or another. But it wasn't the multi-million-dollar waterfront location that made Marina catch her breath, or the sleek yacht moored at the private pier. Instead it was the simpler things—the things that didn't shout out money. Like the small jewel-coloured leadlight window at the end of the hall, the collection of antique pewter in the kitchen, and the rose arbour, filled with the fragrance of summer.

By the time they went upstairs she'd finally lost her stiff formality. Her fingers slid up the curved cedar banister, caressed the marble sculpture positioned in the angle of the corridor, stroked the vibrant petals of a vase of liliums.

Watching avidly, Ronan felt his control fray further. Heat rose to combustible levels. She was so tactile, so sensuous. It was there in her sigh as she breathed in the scent of flowers, her instinctive need to touch.

He wanted those hands on him, knowing his body. Just as he wanted to learn every secret of hers.

He'd realised when they kissed how responsive she was. How dangerous to his control. But nothing had forewarned him about this. He was aroused just watching her sensory pleasure in her surroundings.

'This is your room,' he said, his voice almost brusque at the effort of restraint. He pushed the door open and stood aside, jamming his hands into his pockets as she stepped past him.

'Oh.' Her soft sigh of pleasure enticed him, dragged him into the room behind her.

'It's beautiful. Thank you.' For the briefest of moments her eyes, bright with pleasure, met his. Then she walked forward to investigate, obviously intrigued by the antique furniture.

'My pleasure.' His voice was wooden as he watched her skim the silk coverlet on the bed with her palm. He would *not* think about pushing her down onto its wide expanse, imprinting his naked body on hers.

'There's an *en suite* bathroom.' He gestured to the door in one corner, trying not to envisage her in the enormous spa bath that took up half that room. Or standing nude in front of the massive mirror.

Not yet.

He strode across to the French doors and flung them open. Fresh air, that was what he needed.

'And there's a view from here.' He stared out at the harbour, dark and choppy now as the wind picked up. That must be why the air seemed heavy and close, making breathing difficult. They were in for a summer storm.

'I can't thank you enough.' Her voice came from close beside him. 'You're doing so much for us, for me and Seb.'

He turned. Was that a quiver of emotion in her voice?

She stood watching him, chin up in that characteristically courageous pose. But her eyes gave her away. He didn't miss their bright, over-moist sheen.

And here he'd been, imagining how easy it would be if, in tonight's thunderstorm, Marina needed company. He was only a couple of rooms away, down the corridor or the balcony that so conveniently stretched between their rooms.

Deliberately he drew a steadying breath. Passion had burned white-hot between them whenever he'd taken her in his arms. But clearly this wasn't the time to accelerate their relationship to a more intimate level.

It was support she needed right now. Not sex.

He set his jaw. She was hurting. She'd just lost her father. Had been almost disabled in a horrendous smash. And then she'd had to face the loss of her family enterprise, her livelihood, her home, the future as she knew it.

He curved his lips into a smile that he hoped was reassuring. 'You're helping me achieve something that's long overdue. We're in this together.'

That's it. The scheme against Wakefield. His promise to retrieve her company, make things right for her. If only he'd been able to make things right for Cleo. The knowledge of his failure was like acid, eating away at him.

'Just the same…' she walked past him and onto the balcony '…you've been an enormous help.' She smiled briefly and turned to lean on the balustrade. 'I could never have organised removalists so fast, for a start.'

An unfamiliar pang of conscience shafted through him. It wasn't sympathy that had produced the removalists in record time. It had been sheer selfishness and a hefty wad of cash. He'd wanted Marina here, close by him, so it had happened immediately.

'I have to admit the idea of arranging it all was daunting,' she added.

Ronan watched her swallow, saw the way her mouth turned down at the corners. She'd left the only home she'd known, forced out by her brother's stupidity at a time when she needed care and cosseting. And she'd been thrust into a perilous battle of wills with Charles Wakefield.

It astonished him how angry he felt about that. The tidal surge of protectiveness he felt was totally unexpected. Unprecedented. Except for his response to Cleo's situation. But that was different.

He frowned, perplexed.

Marina was different.

His desire for her, his concern, his total absorption in her, were unlike anything he'd experienced. It wasn't her vulnerability—he'd never been attracted by lame ducks. Or simply her looks—there'd been some stunning beauties in his life. But something about her, something he couldn't put his finger on, drew him like a needle to a magnet.

He had to have her.

And he needed to keep her safe from sharks like Wakefield.

He'd been ready to tell Seb Lucchesi just what he thought of him. The kid needed to grow up, fast. He should be caring for his sister, not relying on her to clean up his fiascos.

But it hadn't been necessary. Reality had hit Seb hard. He'd looked sick with guilt this morning, as he'd helped Marina pack her personal possessions. And it sounded as if he'd been working himself into the ground trying to find some alternative to Wakefield's takeover.

It would do him good to work and worry a little more. But Ronan had been compelled to take him aside and give a sanitised version of his own plans to stop him fussing around Marina, upsetting her. When Seb and his wife had finally left on their trip to visit his in-laws, Marina's relief had been palpable.

Ronan uncurled his white-knuckled fists, fighting the urge to stalk over and wrap her in his arms, pull her close and—

The buzz of his phone sounded and he fished it out of his pocket. The dialler's number was highlighted. It was just the distraction he needed.

'Make yourself at home, Marina. I have to take this call.'

She didn't turn, just nodded and stared out across the garden to the water.

He lifted the phone to his ear as he walked away. 'Hi, babe. How are you?'

Marina watched Ronan cleave through the crowd and out onto the Sydney Opera House terrace, where he could carry on his phone conversation.

It was his sister again. Marina had known the instant he elected to answer the phone. Very few people had that private number, and he answered her calls no matter where he was. He was a caring man, a loving brother, who took his family responsibilities seriously.

The contrast to the indefatigable, implacable businessman still fascinated her.

The first time she'd heard him talk to his sister—the day Marina had moved into his house—she'd thought it was a girlfriend calling. His voice had softened, like rich chocolate, melting right through her defences.

And it had made her jealous as hell!

She'd craved his tender endearments for herself, even then, when she'd hardly known the man. And the sound of his intimate tone, calling some woman 'babe', had made her want to rip the phone out of his hand.

'Your Ronan is a devoted brother.'

Marina turned and looked up at the man to whom she'd just been introduced. Tall, silver-haired and beak-nosed, Sir John Biddulph had a daunting presence. He was obviously one of Ronan's friends, but she wished Ronan hadn't left her alone with him. He looked sharp enough to see through their deception. And without Ronan by her side she felt vulnerable.

'They talk every day,' she said, trying to look relaxed.

'She's away somewhere, isn't she?'

'In Perth.' Marina nodded. 'Having an extended holiday with her mother, I believe.'

'Then it's high time she found a young man of her own to talk to. Ronan should be reserving his attention for you, m'dear, before some other fellow cuts him out.' There was mischief in his smile and a distinct twinkle in his eye, and Marina felt some of her reserve dissolve.

'Ronan tells me you're in freight?'

'Oh?' Ronan had been discussing her? 'Well, yes, but in a very small way.'

'Marina Enterprises, isn't it?'

She nodded, amazed that he knew so much about her. Astounded that Ronan had even mentioned her to him.

'A good sound company. Now, tell me, what do you think of the current fuel excise? How is it affecting your business?'

Discussing the transport industry with Sir John was like a guppy comparing notes with a whale. He was the head of a multinational company and she was—what? Ex-director of an ex-family company?

But his interest seemed genuine and his comments were instructive. Soon Marina forgot the disparity, intrigued by their discussion.

It wasn't until an arm slid round her waist, pulling her close to a solid male body, that she looked round. And lost her breath, as she always did when Ronan came close. The sizzling intensity of his gaze, the tantalising male aroma and that smile. Her train of thought disappeared.

'Don't let me interrupt you.'

'You shouldn't leave this girl on her own, Ronan,' said Sir John. 'Someone unscrupulous, like me, might try to steal her away.'

The sally was gallant and very sweet, considering Sir John had to be pushing seventy.

'You're right, of course. I should have switched off my phone.' Ronan curled his arm further round her, so that his heat scorched through the silk of her gown and she forgot to breathe. 'Intellect and beauty together are a powerful combination. Marina's a very special person.'

Marina felt her eyes boggle. Beauty? Even for a man apparently besotted, wasn't he laying it on too thick? But Sir John merely nodded approvingly.

And then, instead of changing the topic, Ronan steered the

discussion straight back to Marina's last point about duties and charges.

For a moment she was flummoxed. She was used to guys who wanted to hold the floor themselves, cap someone's comment with an even more incisive one of their own.

The conversation lasted another fifteen minutes, till the bell went for them to take their seats. And in that time Ronan didn't try to direct the discussion. He seemed as interested in her opinions as Sir John's. But he didn't humour her.

He made her as if they were equals. That was it.

Marina walked inside, conscious of Ronan's large hand, deliciously warm on her back. And all the while she scoured her memory of their previous conversations.

That was how Ronan always made her feel, she realised.

As if she mattered.

'Marina, are you all right?'

She nodded, keeping her face turned away. 'I'm okay. The carpet's just a little uneven.'

He moved, drawing her arm through his and keeping her close against him. Inevitably she felt it again, that unique, exciting sensation, as if something deep inside her dissolved into a swirl of warm emotion.

But while her body responded her mind was busy, sifting and assessing. Whenever they disagreed he didn't bully her or condescend. He didn't use his wealth and power, or his size, to intimidate her. He always treated her as his equal. Her eyes widened. More than that, he treated her as if she were special.

'After you.' His low voice at her ear made her shiver, and she hurried forward to their allocated seats. When they were settled he linked his fingers with hers, drawing the inevitable response as excitement budded and heat skittered up her arm. As he chatted about the performance they were about to see, Marina's responses were mechanical.

Ronan's attentiveness and charm made her heart race, even though he was simply playing at the role of lover. His strong personality, his integrity and his stunning physical presence were what she'd secretly dreamed of in a partner.

He was the most dangerous man she'd ever met.

With a sinking feeling she turned and looked at him, automatically bracing herself for the impact of his dazzling smile and his intent gaze.

He was gorgeous.

He was out of her league.

Their relationship was pure make-believe.

And she'd just realised she was in serious danger of falling in love with him.

CHAPTER ELEVEN

'COME and have a nightcap?' Ronan asked as he ushered Marina into the house.

'I don't think I—'

'I promise not to bite.'

He watched her eyes widen. Her lips round in a prim circle.

The trouble was, Marina's mouth wasn't at all prim. It was luscious, inviting, seductive. It was enough to give the lie to his statement. For if she stood there much longer, close enough for her delicate scent to waft around him, he'd be tempted to lean over and nibble at her lips until she responded like she had that first night.

A surge of volcanic heat shot through him at the memory of her—so passionate, so responsive in his arms.

Just one taste—

'It's late,' she said, taking a step back.

Immediately frustration clawed at him. She'd been like this almost from the first—blowing hot, then cold. Stoking his libido with her seductive body and smouldering glances. Then pulling back like an ice maiden. But Marina wasn't devious. He was convinced she wasn't playing hard to get.

So what was going on here?

'But you're not tired, are you?' He kept his tone light and cajoling.

Of course she wasn't. Tonight's performance had exhilarated her. That had been obvious from her enthusiastic conversation as they drove home and the unguarded smiles that had slipped past her usual reserve. Her eyes still shone with delight, and she glowed. So, despite his plans to do some late work via e-mail, he found it impossible now to say goodnight and turn away.

'Come on, Marina. You're wide awake. You need time to unwind before you turn in.'

He knew he wouldn't sleep for hours. But that had nothing to do with tonight's world premiere performance and everything to do with the woman before him. She haunted his nights, so tantalisingly close that his body ached at the inhuman restraint he placed on it. He mustn't allow himself to touch. Not yet.

But for how much longer? He couldn't keep this up. And, after all, did he really need to hold back? He could overcome her reserve, obliterate her caution. Seduce her.

Did it really matter that she wasn't yet ready to admit she wanted him? Did it matter that she was still traumatised by recent events?

'Well, I suppose just half an hour. It's been a long day.'

Ronan hoped his answering smile was enigmatic, devoid of the hungry heat that ripped through him, tearing at his resolve. He turned and shepherded her into the sitting room, conscious of her slow steps.

Was she in pain? She never referred to the weakness in her legs but he knew she was still recuperating. From what he'd been able to discover, she was lucky to be walking again.

The thought of her narrow escape still brought him out in a cold sweat.

'What would you like? Liqueur, wine, a soft drink? Or would you prefer coffee?'

'Something light would be good, thanks.'

When he turned from the drinks cabinet she was sitting in a wing chair, looking away from him. Her hand splayed over her skirt, smoothing the soft material.

His attention snapped immediately to the slow movement of her hand. But she didn't look to be in pain. It was a nervous gesture. Instant heat flared, and his temperature soared as he pictured his hand on her leg, sliding up its enticing length. Up the sheer silk of her pantyhose and under her skirt. Or maybe she wasn't wearing pantyhose. Perhaps they were stockings.

He shuddered at the potent eroticism of the image. He could almost feel her warm thighs under his trembling fingers.

He stopped mid-stride and slammed back his drink. Heat scorched down his throat. It was no way to treat an aged single malt.

Marina had no idea how her gesture revealed the long, elegant lines of her legs. How it drew his attention to her innate sensuality.

She was utterly without guile when it came to her body. He'd realised it that first night. She had the body of a seductress, every sensational curve, every long line innately sexy. But she acted as if it was something to hide.

Even now, after days dressed in a wardrobe designed with the sole aim of driving men insane with need, she acted as if she wore a sack. Like the suit he remembered from Wakefield's reception.

How amused Bella Montrose must have been as she'd helped Marina spend his money. He wondered if Bella had any idea what torture he went through now.

'Thank you,' Marina said as she took her drink from his hand. She didn't meet his eyes and, as usual, she was careful not to touch him. He made her uncomfortable.

Uncomfortable!

He'd been in pain since she'd moved in. His whole body was brittle with the strain of self-control. With the agony of repressing lust so incendiary he thought he might self-combust if he couldn't have her soon.

She was driving him crazy.

He dropped in a seat well away from her and put his empty glass on a side table.

'It's a lovely room,' she offered, looking around.

Ah, a nice, polite, pointless conversation. He gritted his teeth, wondering now much longer she could avoid looking at him. 'Thank you.'

'I suppose you got a decorator in to do it?'

'Not a qualified one. At least she isn't yet. My sister did it for me.' At the mention of his sister, some of the fire in his belly faded, replaced with another inevitable tension.

'She's very talented.' And Marina meant it. He could tell by the way her gaze lingered approvingly on the antique Celadon ware in its display alcove, and on the eclectic furniture positioned in comfortable groups. He'd always liked this room, with its elegant proportions and its unparalleled view. But Cleo had transformed it. She really was a genius with interior design.

'Thanks. I'll tell her you like it.'

'You mentioned the other day that she's in Perth. Is she studying there?'

'No.' His voice was too brusque. He saw Marina flinch. 'She's not studying at the moment.'

'Oh. Well, I'm sure there are lots of things to keep her busy there. I've heard it's a lovely city.'

She sipped at her soft drink. She'd given up smoothing her skirt, and fidgeted instead with her tiny beaded purse.

Damn! That was his fault. He hadn't been prepared for her interest in Cleo.

And Cleo had been so interested in Marina, demanding all sorts of details over the phone. She'd even given him permission to tell Marina exactly what Wakefield had done. She'd said Marina needed to hear it, to know what she was up against.

He frowned. He could protect Marina.

Like you protected your sister?

His hands fisted at the recollection of his failure. Guilt pierced him, hollowing his gut.

Was this how he'd feel if Wakefield hurt Marina? He shuddered at the idea. Wakefield couldn't get to Marina now. He'd see to it.

Then he remembered the insistent calls his staff had fielded. The bastard was trying to contact her. And one day he might just succeed.

Tell her, Cleo had urged.

'Ronan, what's wrong?'

He turned his gaze to Marina. She sat up straight in her chair, her eyes huge as she watched him. He felt the tension in his face and knew he'd been scowling.

'Nothing's wrong—' Then he realised the futility of the lie.

If he trusted Marina, if he wanted to protect her, he should tell her the truth. That was what Cleo had said, and he knew she was right.

Yet it went against the grain. The words clogged in his mouth, tasting like betrayal of his sister.

But as he looked into Marina's dark, worried eyes he knew he'd prevaricated long enough. She deserved to know. And he trusted her to keep Cleo's secret. Marina was as honest as anyone he'd ever met.

'It's my sister. Cleo,' he said finally.

'Is she ill?' Marina's smooth brow furrowed.

'She's fine. Now.' He dragged in a deep breath and forced the words out. 'I told you before that Wakefield had hurt a friend of mine.'

Marina nodded, comprehension dawning in her face.

'It wasn't a friend. It was Cleo he hurt.'

'Oh, Ronan!' Her voice was a horrified whisper. 'I'm so sorry.'

He shook his head. It was over. Or almost over. Cleo was so much stronger now. Almost ready to pick up the threads of her life again. It just remained for him to ensure Wakefield got his just desserts. Which meant concentrating on business and not the delicious dilemma now watching him with wide eyes and the most sinful pouting lips imaginable.

'Cleo thought I should tell you what happened.'

'You talked to your sister about me?'

'She wants to meet you. She's got a lot of time for anyone who can see Wakefield for what he is and stand up to him.' A pity Cleo hadn't seen through him earlier.

'You don't have to tell me.' Marina put her glass down on a nearby table, her gaze skating away from his. 'It's private, I know. And it's late. I really should—'

'Stay!' She stiffened and he began again. 'I mean, I'd like you to stay. You need to hear this.'

She slipped back into her chair. A nearby lamp spilled its warm glow over her, picking up the highlights in her glorious hair, revealing the delicate flush of colour high on her cheeks. In that moment Ronan realised that lust was only a fraction of what he felt for this woman. There was a protectiveness and a warmth too, that made him feel—complete.

He held her eyes with his as he spoke, drawing strength from her.

'Last year I spent a few months overseas. I had some negotiations to complete and I was long overdue for a holiday. When I returned…' His hands clenched tight on the arm of his chair. 'When I returned I found Wakefield had given up sniffing around my girlfriends. He'd turned his attentions to my sister instead.'

He should have attacked the bastard then. Taken his fists to him and made him sorry he'd even dared approach her. But life was rarely that simple.

'Cleo is much younger than me. She had no idea of my history with Wakefield, or of what he's really like.' He'd never carried that back to his family. 'She's bright and clever, and full of life, but in some ways naïve.'

Or she had been.

'She was duped by him, completely bowled over. She was in love, and she believed he was too. Nothing anyone said made a difference. She was waiting for his marriage proposal.'

He watched the dawning horror on Marina's face. It echoed his own feelings when he remembered Cleo's face, vivid with excited expectation. The bitter taste of bile rose in his throat at the thought of how much she'd changed since then. Of how much Wakefield had damaged her.

'Ronan?' Marina's voice was low. She perched on the edge of her chair, concern in her expressive eyes.

'The proposal never came,' he said abruptly. 'She discovered she was pregnant instead. She went to him, eager to tell him the news in person. But she never got the words out. That was the day he dumped her, in the cruellest possible way.' His fists grew white-knuckled as scorching fury swept through him.

'He let her find him in bed with another woman. Then he told her their relationship had all been a joke. Just a bit of light relief to see what it was like, screwing Ronan Carlisle's sister.'

He barely registered Marina's outraged exclamation.

Instead it was Cleo's ashen face that riveted his attention. The memory of her, distraught with pain and fear, clutching his hand in a death grip as the doctor confirmed she'd miscarried.

She hadn't cried, not then. She'd been silent and dry-eyed with shock. The tears hadn't come till later. Not till depression had taken her in its grim hold. The downward spiral had been appallingly rapid. The separation from her friends, the insomnia, the burden of self-doubt and, eventually, the desperate bid for release.

His heart pounded against his ribs as he remembered the frantic trip to the hospital, the wait while they pumped her stomach of the sleeping tablets. The crumpled face of his mother as they told her Cleo was lucky to survive.

Marina's skin crawled. Could Wakefield really be that callous?

It would be so much easier to believe Ronan had exaggerated. Except it was no exaggeration. She remembered Wakefield's cold eyes. There had been something inhuman about their icy intensity.

Instinct told her this was the truth, or as much of the truth as Ronan chose to reveal. For it was clear there was more to the story. The expression on his face was so bleak, the pain so real, that she almost reached out to comfort him. His anguish ripped at her. She lifted her hand towards him and then faltered, remembering.

She didn't have the right to comfort him. Their recent intimacy was a charade, and she wasn't really his friend. Her heart plummeted as reality intruded like a blast of white-hot blinding light, forcing her back in her seat.

He wouldn't want her sympathy. She was just another of Wakefield's victims. Ronan had taken her on as a charity case. He'd told her the truth only so she understood the gravity of the situation.

Distress left her wounded and empty.

Even his ferocious scowl and the grooves of pain indenting the corners of his mouth couldn't detract from his charisma. He fascinated her, attracted her, made her feel things she'd never felt before. She wanted to cradle his dark head in her arms and soothe him, ease his hurt. Offer him solace.

Offer herself.

She drew a shuddering, horrified breath.

Even if she found the courage to give herself to him, even if he accepted, she knew he'd be disappointed. He might even be revolted by the sight of her injuries. No, she couldn't bear to see that in his eyes.

'Cleo's been…unwell ever since,' he said, cutting across her thoughts.

'And the baby?' She dreaded the answer.

'A miscarriage.'

Marina sank back against the cushioned upholstery, feeling sick to her stomach. She stared out of the window towards the harbour lights. But all she saw was the fierce pain and hot fury in Ronan's eyes.

'Doesn't Wakefield *expect* you to act against him?' He'd be the world's biggest fool if he didn't. 'After what he did to your sister—'

Ronan shook his head. 'Wakefield's not sure I know about that. Cleo may not have confided in me. And he certainly doesn't know about the pregnancy.' He looked across at her with glittering, unreadable eyes.

'But it's my responsibility to stop him before anyone else gets hurt.' His mouth was a severe line, his jaw set implacably. It was obvious nothing could sway him from his purpose.

Now it all made sense. His obsessive need to obliterate Wakefield. His willingness to champion her cause against a common enemy. Ronan's protectiveness. Even the scorchingly intense looks.

It wasn't attraction he felt for her. She'd always known that with her head. But in her heart had lurked a secret, stupid hope. She felt it wither at last, shrivel to nothing inside her.

Ronan saw her as another vulnerable woman.

She probably reminded him of his sister.

He'd decided she was weak and helpless. A poor, homeless, injured victim. Someone who couldn't take care of herself and needed protecting from a rapacious wolf like Charles Wakefield.

She bit back a sob of despair at the futility of those secret longings she'd clutched to her heart. How foolish she'd been, even to dream there might be something more between them.

Ronan pitied her.

CHAPTER TWELVE

MARINA turned in the water and pushed off from the end of the pool. A couple more laps and she'd quit. Ronan wouldn't be home for hours, even though the shadows were lengthening. But she always played it safe and finished her swim well before he arrived home.

Whenever he was near she needed her wits about her, ready to repress her traitorous reactions.

To her dismay, she'd discovered her weakness for him grew stronger each day. He only had to walk into a room, or look at her in a certain way, to make her pulse gallop and her breath shorten.

Mercifully, they hadn't played their charade often. There'd been the opening night at the Opera House, another cocktail party, and a few dinners at expensive restaurants. Each time he'd been the perfect attentive lover. His arm around her had been like a brand, a searingly exquisite mark of possession that she enjoyed far too much. His show of solicitous interest came so easily she almost believed it was real.

Even here in his home, where they didn't pretend, he made her long for what she couldn't have. He didn't encroach on her space. It wasn't his fault she yearned for a reprise of their passionate kisses. Or that the knowledge that he slept just two doors away kept her awake through the long, hot summer nights. Awake and wanting.

She knew he felt not one iota of desire for her. Yet that knowledge didn't have the power to blunt her craving.

The idea of playing his lover filled her with excitement and apprehension.

She couldn't imagine deceiving his close friends. Someone was sure to spot her as a fake. She had the glamorous clothes, and she didn't wobble any more in high heels. But the woman beneath the gloss was just the same as before. Ordinary. Scarred.

So it was strange how, when Ronan was at her side, smiling down at her, she felt anything but average. Felt almost pretty.

Who did she think she was kidding?

Her palm slapped against the tiles at the end of the pool and she lifted her head, heaving in a deep breath. She needed oxygen. Too much thinking about Ronan and not her pacing. She let herself slide under the water. But closing her eyes didn't obliterate the image of his sexy smile.

She bobbed to the surface. A hand, well-shaped and large, appeared before her. She looked up into Ronan's face and caught her breath at the intensity of his gaze.

'Come on.' His deep voice had a rough edge. 'It's time you got out of there.'

Ignoring his outstretched hand, she propelled herself back from the wall, automatically seeking safety in distance. No man had the right to look so good in business clothes, with his sleeves rolled up over tanned, sinewy forearms and the top buttons of his shirt undone.

'I'm not finished,' she panted. Anything to get him to leave.

His brows drew together. 'Yes, you are. Mrs Sinclair said you've been out here for forty minutes.'

'You set your housekeeper to spy on me?' Marina had liked the woman, with her easy manner and no-nonsense attitude, and felt disappointed.

'Don't be absurd. She happened to notice when you went out, and she's concerned you don't have a relapse. She knows you're recuperating.'

Feeling stupid, Marina concentrated on treading water, ignoring his hand still imperiously outstretched.

'I'll be out in a minute,' she said. 'I'll see you inside.'

'You'll get out now.' This time it was an order. 'Look at your breathing, woman. You need to stop.'

Her chest was heaving, it was true. But it was as much to do with the effect he had on her as the exercise.

'I said I'd get out soon.' After he'd gone safely indoors and she had some privacy. It was bad enough when strangers at the local public pool stared at her. She didn't need that from Ronan.

'Marina.' His voice was a low growl that sent a message of primal power. 'Take my hand now, and let me help you out, or I'll come in and get you.'

She opened her mouth to protest that he wouldn't be so stupid, not when he was fully clothed. But one look at the grim set of his mouth convinced her it was no idle threat.

Still she hesitated, and in that moment his hands went to his shirt, rapidly unbuttoning, his eyes holding hers.

'Okay,' she all but shouted, feeling ridiculous now. 'I'm coming out.'

Instead of gripping his hand, she swam to the side of the pool, keeping her left side away from him. Then she grabbed the ladder and hauled herself up. He was right, she realised with annoyance. She'd swum too long and her legs were trembling. But she'd make it to the sun-lounge and her towel.

He was there before her, walking towards her with a towel held out in both arms.

She stiffened as his gaze swept over her, briefly but comprehensively. Heat rose in her cheeks as she pictured what he saw. She barely resisted the temptation to cover the ugly scars that marred her left thigh. But it was too late, and they were too massive to conceal.

She lifted her chin to stare squarely into his face. His closed expression gave nothing away, neither distaste nor pity. But his eyes seemed darker than usual, almost stormy with emotion. She supposed he wasn't used to anyone crossing him.

He made no comment on the disfiguring legacy of her car crash, and she was too proud to refer to it. Right now it was only stiff pride that kept her upright. The swim and the stupid confrontation had sapped all her energy.

She took a step towards him, her hand reaching for the towel, and one leg buckled. She recovered quickly, shifting her weight to her other foot so she could balance again.

But not fast enough. In a single stride Ronan closed the

distance between them and swept her up into his arms, towel and all. His swearing, low-voiced and pithy, sounded just above her head.

'There's no need for that. I can stand.' Her protest was an indignant hiss.

'There's every need,' he countered, as he pulled her dripping body closer and swung round towards the house.

She stared at the set line of his jaw, at the tension in his strong neck, and knew she should be wishing herself anywhere but here in his arms. Even though excitement fizzed through her bloodstream and the inevitable tendrils of forbidden desire unfurled low in her abdomen.

He strode across the wide paved courtyard and through an open door, kicking it shut behind them with a savagery that made it crash. The sound reverberated through the house.

Her stomach clenched in a mixture of fear and exhilaration, and she shivered. Surely she wasn't enjoying the sight of Ronan, the most controlled, unreadable man she'd ever met, losing his cool.

She had to get a grip.

'Ronan,' she said as calmly as she could, trying to ignore the rapid thump of his heartbeat near her ear and the spicy male scent of him teasing her senses. 'You're right. I should have got out earlier. But you don't need to do this. I can walk.'

'Perhaps I enjoy carrying you.' His voice was sharp, impatient. 'Did you ever consider that?'

Marina hadn't. Couldn't conceive of it. And her mind boggled at the possibility.

She darted a look at his face, reading only annoyance in his furrowed brow and the tight line of his mouth.

Surely he didn't mean it. Even to a man of his size she'd be a burden. He felt sorry for her, that was all. Was worried she'd fall flat on her face.

The trouble was that, cradled in his arms, she felt cherished and ridiculously feminine in a way that was far removed from her usual assertive style.

Even that first night when he'd held her, she'd been ready to drop from exhaustion and bitter defeat, but there'd been magic in his embrace.

He hitched her closer, his arms like warm steel and his hands splayed wide against her wet body. His touch generated a heat that seared and spread through every vein.

With a sigh of surrender she gave in to the inevitable. She let her head relax against him, her hands curve into his hard muscles as he carried her up the stairs.

She shut her eyes and, despite her better judgement, concentrated on collecting a memory of the moment. One she could savour when she was alone again. There was the steady rhythm of his steps ascending the long sweep of staircase. The reverberating thud of his heart beating in the wide wall of his chest. The aroma of him, stronger than the tang of salty pool water, curling around her. The tension of his bunched muscles beneath her fingers.

Face it, Marina, you've got it bad.

He shouldered his way through a door and her eyes flew open at the sound of it slamming shut behind them.

She looked up to see the delicate plaster tracery of the ceiling in her room. And then he strode across to the four-poster bed and lowered her, half dropping her, onto it.

'The bedspread,' she protested, scrabbling to find purchase to lever herself up and off the exquisite silk bedcovering.

'Damn the bedspread.' With one large hand he pushed against her shoulder so she flopped back onto the mattress.

'What the hell did you think you were doing, Marina? Or didn't you think?' He loomed over her, eyes sparking. 'Don't you care that you might do yourself an injury? Cause a relapse that could undo all the work the surgeons have done?'

Her mouth opened, but no words came out. She was transfixed by the sight of Ronan Carlisle, his face stripped of its usual veneer of urbane sophistication. She'd wondered time and again what he was hiding behind his mask of control. Now she had her wish.

Pure, unadulterated fury blazed at her. It was there in the glitter of his darkened eyes and the flare of his nostrils. His feet were planted wide apart in a stance that radiated machismo. Tension corded his neck, and his hands alternately fisted and unclenched at his sides, as if seeking an outlet in action.

And she wanted him.

Big, angry, utterly masculine in his thwarted fury, but he didn't scare her. She knew he'd never hurt her. He wasn't that sort of man.

Instead, the sight of him physically battling such strong emotion stoked the spiral of excitement and need in her own traitorous body. It was all she could do not to squirm beneath his hot stare, revel in the sensations he evoked.

She had to be depraved. Turned on by his anger? Where had that come from?

Marina shook her head, trying to dredge up some sanity from the fog of emotions that deprived her of common sense.

She struggled to keep her breathing even. 'I'm okay. I just took the laps too quickly and—'

'And nothing! It's a good thing I came home when I did, or I could have found you floating face-down in the water.'

'Oh, don't be ridiculous,' she snapped, forgetting her resolution to be calm in the face of his overreaction.

'Ridiculous, is it?' He bent close to glare at her. 'And I suppose you weren't being ridiculous when you refused to get out of the pool?'

'I can make my own decisions.' She propped herself up on one arm, refusing to take this lying down. 'I'm a grown woman, in case you'd forgotten.'

His bitter laugh sent a puff of warm air across her face. 'I haven't forgotten, Marina. Believe me.' He paused to drag his gaze from her face, down her body, to her legs.

Immediately warmth, the telltale pooling of desire, welled low in her belly. Her nipples hardened and puckered, so that it took every ounce of willpower not to draw attention to them further by covering her breasts with her hands.

'And I suppose you thought it made sense to stay in the water rather than let me see this?'

He lowered his hand to her left thigh. It wasn't the tentative touch of a fingertip tracing the unsightly scar tissue. It was the solid warmth of his whole palm, flat across her wet skin, long fingers splayed to cover the mess of her injuries.

She flinched and caught her breath.

His hand slid round her thigh, caressing the worst of the scars she'd tried so obstinately to keep from his view.

'Don't!' The word choked her.

'Why not?' His eyes were on hers, reading the emotion she couldn't hide. 'You've got to face it some time, Marina. It's part of you now, and you have to learn to live with it.'

Tears of sheer fury blurred the lines of his face and she blinked rapidly to clear her vision.

'You arrogant bastard! Don't you think I know that? I lived with the pain of it for months. How am I supposed to forget when I see it every time I shower? Every time I dress? I feel the weakness and I remember…'

Her throat closed as memories came rushing back. Being in the car with her father—the last time she'd seen him alive. The banshee screech of the truck's brakes as it slewed straight into them on the wet road, tossing their car end for end.

And now this man, who knew nothing about the pain of losing someone so tragically, or how it felt to be disfigured, had the hide to preach to her because she wanted to preserve what little dignity she could muster.

She glared at him, not knowing at that moment which was stronger—her need for him, or the wish never to see him again.

'You don't understand.' Her voice was hoarse.

'Oh, sweetheart, I understand all right.' His words were a whisper of breath against her forehead as he leaned close and stroked his hand gently from her cheekbone to her chin.

There was tenderness in the rough timbre of his voice and in his feather-light touch. And she knew it would be her undoing. She could cope with anything but that.

Spurred by the need to wrest some control again, by the anger that hadn't abated, she shoved his caressing hand away. Grabbing his shoulders, she pulled herself up and kissed him—right on the mouth.

Not with tenderness or subtlety. But with all the roiling mass of conflicting emotions that surged through her: anger, grief, despair and longing. Her mouth was urgent, hard with desperation against the pliant warmth of his lips. She barely felt the strain in her neck and arms at holding herself inches above the bed, clinging to the solid, real strength of him.

And he let her kiss him, tilted his head to accommodate her. But he didn't kiss her back, not properly.

He was letting her use him. He felt sorry for her, and was letting her work off her pain and frustration on him.

Damn him! She was *not* an object of pity. She wouldn't let herself be.

She slid her hands from his shoulders to the back of his head, allowing herself to fall back against the bed as she did so.

For a minute she felt resistance in his strong frame, his wide shoulders unyielding despite the tug of her weight against him. And then, at last, her urgency won out. He allowed her to pull him down. His body covered hers.

Marina barely noticed the way he braced himself on his arms so as not to crush her. She only knew that he was here with her, the taste of him enticing, the feel of his hard strength inciting her kiss to transform from furious to passionate.

Her fingers thrust through his silky hair, splayed over his skull. She tugged at his bottom lip, nipped it with her teeth, and then tasted him with her tongue. His lips parted and at last she delved into the haven of his mouth.

Her hands gentled, cupped his head, and she sighed, realising how completely she wanted him. The clean musky scent of him excited her. The feel of his long body blanketing hers was comforting and unsettling. She twisted beneath him, revelling in the sensations.

And then in a heartbeat it all changed.

He came alive in her arms.

Like an unstoppable force he drove her down against the mattress. The kiss she'd thought she controlled turned into a lush, achingly sensuous, fiery mating of their mouths. She hung on to him desperately, afraid to lose her one point of reference in their dizzying passion.

He surged against her, no longer passive but arrogantly masterful. He thrust her legs apart with one knee, pushing them wider so he could plant himself intimately in the cradle of her hips. The soft friction of expensive pure wool suiting against the sensitive flesh of her inner thighs, the weighted hardness of him pressing down against her, brought a gasp of awareness to her lips.

And a rough growl to his. It rumbled in his throat and vibrated against her bruised mouth.

And still she couldn't get enough.

She moved beneath him, urgent in her need to get closer. As close as it was possible to get to this man who filled her every sense. He eclipsed her mind so that nothing mattered but the passion that bound them.

One large marauding hand palmed her hair, spanned her throat, skimmed her bare shoulder, then slid unerringly to cup her breast. He squeezed gently and every muscle in her body stiffened as darts of sizzling heat shot through her. His thumb brushed her nipple once, twice, and a jolt of pure desire shook her. She ached for more.

And he gave it. He released her mouth, lowering his head in a trickle of kisses down her jaw, across the ultra-sensitive flesh of her neck, then, as if impatient himself, directly to her other nipple, laving it through the slick Lycra.

She sucked in a gasp of air for her oxygen-starved brain. But thought was impossible as she watched his dark head bent over her, his mouth and hand on her breasts. The feel of his teeth nipping at her was exquisite torment.

And through it all the lava-hot flow of desire swirled and centred deep in her body, throbbed between her legs.

She pushed up against him and was rewarded with the solid weight of his own need thrusting hard against her. It soothed the ache of emptiness, but only for a moment. Even that wasn't enough now.

Disjointed thoughts swirled through her mind, but she couldn't make them connect. Not when Ronan, the man she'd dreamed about since their first meeting, was doing such outrageously wonderful things to her. With her.

When his hand slipped from her breast along the taut line of her body to her thigh, she struggled to breathe. And when his hand moved, firm and deliberate, from her bare thigh to the thin fabric between her legs, she thought her heart might stop.

His fingers spread and swirled and rubbed till she strained up to meet his touch.

'Ronan,' she murmured. Her voice was unrecognisable, husky with longing. She wanted so much from him. More than she'd ever let herself admit. More than he'd ever know.

'Mmm?' He kissed up her throat, along to the base of her ear.

And then, as if he knew exactly what she wanted, his long fingers slipped beneath the edge of the Lycra, insinuating themselves across the tender skin of her belly and dipping down to the core of her heat.

'Ronan!'

Helpless, in the grip of sensations stronger than she'd ever encountered, she felt her body lift to his touch, begging for more.

And again he met her need. His hand slid down until his fingers probed, circled, and entered.

'Don't!' she panted. Frantic thoughts whirled in her head. It was what she wanted. But it wasn't. She wanted more. She wanted him. All of him.

But his caress was deliberate, rhythmic, and she moved restlessly against his stroking hand.

'Don't what?' His words were hot in her mouth. His lips demanding against hers.

And suddenly she felt the world tilt and slide. There was a roaring in her ears, a dazzle of bursting light. Her body stiffened, pulled taut by a surge of unbelievable sensation.

'Don't…stop,' she gasped as he took her mouth with his and brought her to glorious, mind-numbing ecstasy.

She shuddered uncontrollably, held close in his embrace.

It was long minutes before she surfaced from the spiral of physical and emotional intensity. A lifetime before she came back to herself, aware of her body, sated and pliant beneath his. Of his mouth, gentle against her neck. His heartbeat, throbbing fast within his chest. The unmistakable rigidity of an aroused male, tense and unfulfilled, above her.

Tentatively she raised a weighted hand to stroke the firm line of his jaw and he froze. She felt his sudden inhalation against her skin.

He shifted his weight, moved his leg over hers, and her breath caught. Despite the wonderful climax he'd given her, she was wanton enough to want more. She yearned for the physical completion that no one but he could give. She needed him. And it was obvious that he wanted her.

Make love to me, Ronan.

That was what she wanted to say.

But she knew he wouldn't want to hear that from her.

'I want you,' was what she whispered.

He froze above her, and even his breathing seemed to stop.

Tentatively she slid her hand down his body, past the finely woven shirt, the sleek leather belt, the soft wool of his trousers, till her hand closed round him, long and hard and inviting.

Oh, Lord.

'No!' He reared back, pushing her hand away and bracing himself at arm's length above her. His wide shoulders blotted out the room and she felt almost small, and very vulnerable beneath him.

She frowned, unable to decipher anything beyond the feverish glitter in his eyes. Wasn't she supposed to touch him?

'But you haven't…' Her words petered out as his expression settled into grim lines.

'That doesn't matter.' He looked as if he was gritting his teeth.

'But…' She bit her lip, wondering what she'd done wrong. She lifted her hands to cup his jaw, feeling the infinitesimal abrasion of his burgeoning stubble.

'Please, Ronan.'

She was beyond pride now. He must know how she felt. How infatuated she was with him. She had nothing more to lose.

'Please,' she whispered. 'I want you inside me.'

This close, she could see the way his pupils dilated, feel the way his jaw clenched in violent spasm. And then he was pushing himself up on his arms, away from her.

Bereft of his heat, she shivered. Or maybe it was because of the shuttered expression in his eyes. It wasn't the look of a lover. Or even a friend.

They were a stranger's eyes.

'No,' he said, thrusting himself to his feet. His eyes swept her body once, comprehensively, then he jerked his head round to look out of the window. 'You don't know what you're asking.'

But suddenly, shatteringly, she knew exactly what she'd been asking. She bit her lip hard, hoping the pain would help her concentrate on keeping the tears at bay.

She'd fallen in love with him. Had been hiding from the truth for days. Pretending that love at first sight wasn't a family weakness despite the way it had struck both her parents and Seb.

Despite all her efforts, all her stern self-admonition, she'd succumbed to the fantasy. Had fallen under the spell of the role she played and Ronan's irresistible attraction. She'd drifted into a pleasant daydream where Ronan cared for her. Had even deluded herself that the flare of heat she sometimes discerned in his eyes was desire. She'd succumbed to the pathetic fairytale: her as the beautiful maiden and Ronan as the handsome prince who rescued her.

But it was pity he felt for her. Pity and, judging by his expression when he'd just looked at her, distaste for the way she looked. For the grotesque scars she couldn't hide.

You don't know what you're asking.

She rolled over on her side, so he couldn't see her face crumple.

He'd been angry that she might have put herself in danger. He'd been sorry for her because of the damage to her body on top of everything else. He felt responsible in some way for her.

He hadn't caressed her out of desire. Or anything remotely like love. She supposed the aroused state of his body was a simple male reaction to watching a woman climax in his arms.

She blinked furiously and burrowed her face into the bedspread. He'd taken pity on her, but he didn't want her.

And who could blame him?

Despite the new look and the expensive clothes she was still the same old Marina. She'd been kidding herself.

Nothing had really changed.

The truth was so devastating she didn't even hear him stride out of the room and leave her alone.

CHAPTER THIRTEEN

HE WAS on fire.

His chest heaved, about to burst. His skin stretched too tight. His breathing was a harsh rattle in his throat.

He gripped the basin of the *en suite* bathroom with both hands, striving for control. Then he wrenched on the tap, bent low and soused his head. He rubbed the cold water down his neck, scrubbed his face with it, let it beat down on him.

It did no good. His need was still a physical pain, throbbing through his body. So strong it made his teeth ache.

He shut off the tap and straightened, flicking water from his hair, feeling it trickle down from his neck and shoulders.

His reflection met him as he stood up. Shirt half unbuttoned and soaked. Hands unsteady. Eyes almost black with lust. Facial features taut, pared down to stark lines of raw desire.

I want you inside me.

He groaned. Marina hadn't known what she was asking.

A decent man would walk away. As he'd done.

A decent man would put those words from his mind.

But he couldn't.

I want you.

The words echoed in his brain, growing louder, not softer.

A decent man would remember that she was hurting. Grieving. That she needed protection, even from herself, as she struggled to re-establish her equilibrium and salvage her damaged pride in the face of others' pity.

A truly decent man would know that it was her bruised ego talking and wouldn't take advantage.

But his reflection wasn't that of a decent man. Though he'd tried, heaven help him. He'd worked long hours on his scheme to bring Wakefield undone and it was succeeding. The moment of triumph drew closer each day. But it was a hollow victory when he knew the real reason for his compulsive drive was to avoid the temptation that had taken up residence in his home. Marina.

Having her in the house had been his own brilliant idea, but now she was here he'd discovered, too late, how dangerous she was. Like a glass of wine set before an alcoholic, she was pure temptation.

He thought of her passionate mouth and groaned. Her fiery eyes and soft-as-seduction hair. Her quick mind and determination. Her independence, that wouldn't let her be cowed by a rich bastard like Wakefield. Or by him. Her body, ripe and lush with its hourglass figure no man could resist.

He turned away, knowing he was no longer a decent man.

She was still on the bed when he returned. Her eyes were bleak as she stared out of the window. Her legs were tucked up and her wet hair spilled like a protective shield around her hunched shoulders. She looked so vulnerable.

He should do the right thing—turn his back and leave her alone.

Her head jerked round when he stalked across to the bed, eyes widening as he threw the packet of condoms onto the bedside table.

'No!' She pushed herself up from the bedspread. 'I didn't mean it. I don't want you to…'

The rest of her words were lost in the heavy rush of blood in his ears that half-deafened him. And the sound of his shirt ripping.

His hands were on his belt when she found her voice again. 'Ronan, no. I don't want this.'

He kicked off his shoes as he undid his trousers and let them fall.

'Are you sure?' His voice was a husky growl. Definitely not the sound of a decent man. Or even a reasonable one.

Stepping away from his discarded clothes, he bent to peel off his socks and heard the hiss of her indrawn breath.

When he straightened she was reaching towards him, her hand half raised. His breath jammed in his chest as she leaned forward. Her lips were sultry invitation, her breasts superb, her body meant for his.

'What's that?' Her words were almost inaudible over the hammering beat of his heart.

He twisted round and saw realisation freeze her features, as he had known it would.

'It's scar tissue, Marina.' He stared at her, challenging her. 'Is it so ugly you can't bear to make love to me?'

'Of course not!'

She hadn't thought that one through. But he didn't mind as she scooted forward on the bed and he felt the tentative brush of her fingers at his side. He shuddered and prayed for control.

'What happened?'

'Like you,' he said harshly. 'An accident. But mine was a plane crash. Our Cessna went down in the bush.' He felt her warm palm slide around to his back, spreading hesitantly over the burn mark that marred his skin. 'I was twenty and my best mate was twenty-one. He was the pilot and he died in the smash.'

'Oh, Ronan.'

'Save your pity.' Right now he wasn't interested in reliving the loss of his friend, or his three-day fight for survival in the wilderness.

Right now his mind was fixed on one thing. Marina. And how good this was going to be.

'So you *do* know.'

'What?' He frowned, trying to follow her words.

'You do know what it's like,' she repeated, her hand a soft caress across his skin. 'Loss,' she explained. 'And injury.'

He grabbed her wrist and pulled her hand away from him. He couldn't take much more. Not if he was going to retain any shred of control. Already the tension in his strained muscles had ratcheted almost to breaking point.

He planted his hand against her shoulder and pushed her back against the pillows. She looked like a stranded, sexy mermaid. All that long glossy hair spreading across the bed. Her eyes so wide he could drown in their velvet depths. Her lips parted in a naturally seductive pout that made his muscles spasm.

Pure sexual bliss beckoned. Already he knew the taste of her and the petal-soft feel of her bare skin. The sweet scent of her arousal. The erotic little cries of her ecstasy. And her raw, unfettered responsiveness to his touch, the biggest turn-on of them all.

'Now's not the time for that discussion,' he managed to say over the tightness in his chest. He shoved down his boxers and reached for the box on the bedside table.

'The only thing that matters right now, Marina, is how badly I want you. And from the look on your face I know you feel the same.'

He paused long enough for her to protest. But she didn't. Instead she watched him with a mixture of longing and awe that would have been a treat for his ego if he hadn't been in such pain.

He sheathed himself and knelt on the bed before her, slowly closing the distance between them. She gulped, then licked her lips as if her mouth was dry, but she didn't retreat.

'Take it off,' he whispered.

She fumbled at the straps of her one-piece swimsuit, dragging it jerkily from her shoulders. She struggled with it, hunching a shoulder to manoeuvre the slick material down. Then her arms were free.

'All the way,' he ordered, holding her gaze. Her eyes were wide with shock and excitement.

Slowly she bared one creamy breast, and then the other. They were just as he'd imagined. Perfect. Proud and full and utterly seductive.

She shimmied, pushing the wet cloth lower. The suspense became too much. He reached out, ripped the black fabric away in one surge of violent energy and tossed the swimsuit across the room.

He heard her gasp. His own breath stopped somewhere in his aching chest.

She was beautiful. Sultry, sexy curves. The enticing dip to her waist. The feminine flare of hips just meant to cradle him against her body. Glossy dark curls below a tiny belly. Long, long, shapely legs. His hand hovered over her, close but not touching. If he touched he'd be lost before he even started.

He darted a look at her face, wondering if she knew what she'd just unleashed. But her eyes weren't on his face. She was looking lower, and he throbbed in response.

Was that anxiety he read in her face?

'Lie down.' His voice was strangled, a rough whisper, but she understood and settled herself back on the bed.

He moved up to straddle her, knees on either side of her hips, and lifted a hand to her face. She was trembling and his heart squeezed.

'It'll be all right, Marina,' he promised, wondering how the hell he'd salvage the willpower to make it right for her.

She raised a hand to his heaving chest and he shuddered. Heat seared his skin, radiating from her touch and sparking a potent erotic response. Right now he couldn't withstand her caresses.

He captured both her wrists and lifted them above her head, gripping them lightly in one hand, watching the way the movement tilted her body slightly, raising her breasts towards him invitingly. His tension notched up unbearably as he reminded himself he had to share, not ravage.

Unsteadily he settled himself beside her, shivering at the sensation of her soft skin against him. He let one thigh splay over hers, pushing them wide.

Her breasts rose and fell with her rapid breathing, but he didn't dare suckle them, not now. Instead he cupped her intimately with his palm, grinding the heel of his hand against the sensitive spot between her legs so that her hips bucked and she pushed against him. His fingers slid against her, feeling the slickness of her arousal. He could smell her musky, feminine scent. Soon, he promised himself.

She shifted, trying to break his grasp. 'Ronan, please,' she gasped. 'Ronan…'

'Shh. I know, honey. You want more. So do I.'

He rolled over, positioning himself above her, revelling in the embrace of her satiny thighs encompassing him. Molten heat flared deep inside as he nudged at the very core of her and looked into her eyes. What he saw there made him feel like a king. And her pliant, welcoming woman's body beneath his was all the enticement he needed.

Releasing her hands, he braced himself above her as he slowly, inexorably, thrust forward.

Oh, God. It was heaven and hell combined. Ecstasy and torture. She was so tight, so—

His brow furrowed. She couldn't be…

He stopped, quivering from the effort of holding back, and tried to force his mind to work.

Her face was drawn in stark lines. Whether of delight or pain he couldn't tell. But she was tensed, her whole body taut as if in shock. Her breath came shallowly, pushing her breasts up against him in an agitated rhythm.

Taking his weight on one arm, he brushed a shaking hand across her collarbone, down the fine porcelain skin of her breast, to skim her dusky nipple. She shuddered and her breath caught. But still she kept her beautiful eyes shut, as if trying to block him out.

He stroked her breast with his whole hand, cupping its feminine weight, then slid lower to kiss her there. Immediately her heady, unique fragrance filled his nostrils. She tasted so sweet. He loved the way she trembled at the deliberately slow lap of his tongue against her nipple.

'Ronan.' It was a throaty whisper of need. He smiled against her breast, sure of himself now. He let himself concentrate on enjoying her breast under his tongue, licking, kissing, sucking.

'Ronan!' More desperate this time. He felt her hands slide down him, restless and seeking. She smoothed over his back, trying to draw him up again. He hooked an arm under her knee, tilting her hips up to him and slid forward, deep into the waiting warmth of her.

Her eyes opened then: wide, bright and dazed. But their expression was welcoming, wanting, and he knew it was all right now.

'Marina.' He'd never felt it before: savage wanting paired with such tenderness, such a need to give her everything. She was so much more than he'd ever imagined.

He lowered his head to kiss the frenetic pulse in her neck and she shuddered. Her hands went to his shoulders, fingers splayed, gripping possessively. He moved infinitesimally and her hips rose to him in an invitation he couldn't refuse. He rocked against her and she met him. Again. And again.

Her breathing was a raw rasp in his ear. She lifted her knees higher, wrapping her long, gorgeous legs around him, holding on tight as his movements quickened. He almost lost it then, aware of her silken body everywhere against his.

He struggled to control the pace, not race to completion as his body urged. But soon he heard his name on her lips, felt her contract around him, pulsing and drawing him further and faster. That was when he let himself go in the sheer, mindless ecstasy of making love to Marina.

And through the mind-numbing barrage of sensations and turbulent emotions—triumph, fulfilment, and finally exhaustion—he realised he'd been right all the time. Nothing could rival making love to Marina Lucchesi.

Afterwards, limbs weighted and drowsy, he just managed to roll off her. His arms bound her fast to him, pulling her close as he settled on his back. Her hair, still damp, spread over him like a mermaid's tresses. Her warm body, hazed with sweat like his, sprawled in utter abandon.

No, he hadn't been a decent man.

Lord help them both. He hadn't cared about what was right. Just about satisfying that blood-hot craving.

She'd been a virgin. Against all odds he'd been her first. The very idea of it still dazed him.

And the realisation filled him with a wholly masculine thrill of ownership. He felt his lips curve in a self-satisfied smile he couldn't prevent. His hand skimmed possessively over her body, down her smooth back to the seductive curve of her hip. No one but he had touched her like this. The realisation was such a turn-on that he had to force his thoughts away.

She'd been trusting and, despite her sassy front, hurting badly. Needing his care, relying on his honour to help and protect her.

But he'd failed her. He hadn't been honourable. Hadn't protected her. Instead he'd been completely, inexcusably selfish, taking advantage of her weakness when she was most vulnerable. He should be ashamed of himself. He waited for the arrow-sharp pang of conscience to hit him.

But it didn't come. Instead he felt a smug satisfaction that he had exactly what he needed.

She didn't know he'd wanted her from the first. Had wanted to help her almost as much as he'd wanted her in his bed.

He let his fingers trail possessively over her fine skin, already planning their next sensual encounter. After he'd given her time to recover.

He'd guessed at the start she was different, special. And how right he'd been!

One thing was clear—he couldn't make love to her once and walk away.

For as long as this incandescent passion burned bright between them Marina would be his lover.

CHAPTER FOURTEEN

MARINA woke to the slide of soft silk being drawn over her. She sighed and burrowed her head into the pillow, emerging slowly from sleep.

Her body was alive in ways it had never been before. She revelled in the weighted sensation of fulfilment and in the tingling hint of expectation in her blood.

She felt wonderful, completed. And all because of Ronan. The man who'd made her feel beautiful, desirable, special. As if she really *was* the woman of his dreams. As he was the embodiment of all her longings.

Tentatively she reached out to caress him, slip her hand across the solid warmth of his chest. She needed the reassurance of his embrace to remind her that this was no dream. But her fingers found only the empty bed, still warm from his body.

It couldn't be.

Frantically she swiped her arm out as far as she could reach.

A dart of something like panic jabbed her. But when she opened her eyes she found it was true. She was alone in the darkening room.

He'd even closed the door when he left.

Her chest squeezed and she swallowed against the hard lump of distress that lodged in her throat. For the second time that day unaccustomed tears filmed her eyes.

What had she expected? A declaration of love? A promise of for ever?

Her lips compressed bitterly at her own stupidity.

At least he'd shown the common decency to cover her naked body when he went.

Hell! She screwed up her eyes against the flood of despair. What had she done?

On a surge of bitter energy she slid off the bed to stand, swaying with shock and the effort of holding back her pain. Life had taught her not to believe in miracles. So why was she surprised that he'd taken what she'd offered—what she'd pleaded for—and then walked away?

Marina pulled the silken cover up and around her with trembling fingers, needing its warmth against her chilled body. It trailed heavily behind her as she stumbled towards her private bathroom.

She averted her eyes from the sight of her swimsuit, torn asunder and crumpled in two pathetic heaps by the window.

She knew exactly what she'd done.

She tugged the voluminous coverlet through the door, then snicked shut the lock. Sighing, she dropped the bedspread and yanked on the shower tap. Instantly steam rose and she stepped under the spray, gasping at the heat and reaching to adjust it.

She'd given herself to Ronan Carlisle. Begged him, offered herself so shamelessly that he'd overcome his distaste and his scruples to take her. They'd had sex.

But she'd made love.

She'd been a fool. A ridiculous, pathetic fool. She prayed that he hadn't guessed the truth about her feelings.

Feelings. Hah! Such an insipid word. She had feelings of affection for friends and neighbours. Feelings of tenderness and regard. But her emotions for Ronan were like a whirlpool, a surging, tugging vortex of pressure that overwhelmed her in spite of every last shred of common sense and self-preservation.

She bent her head and let the drumming water wash down over her entire body as if it could wash away this fatal weakness in her.

For even now, faced with the brutal truth, she couldn't honestly say she regretted what had happened. It had been wonderful. Ardent and exciting and downright earth-shattering. His power. His almost unwilling tenderness. His passion. The strength and beauty of him. She'd revelled in it all.

Despite his lack of true feeling for her he'd made her feel like a queen.

She'd loved it. And she wanted more.

That made her sick in anyone's book.

He hadn't lured her with soft words or false promises. He couldn't have made it clearer that he didn't want a relationship. He'd walked away rather than face her.

But there was no denying what they'd shared was wonderful.

Imagine what making love with Ronan would be like if he felt for her as she did for him.

No! She wasn't masochist enough to go there. She couldn't afford to let herself dream the impossible. Unrequited love was bad enough. She couldn't afford to live in a fantasy world any longer, deluding herself that wishes might come true.

She turned off the water and stepped out of the shower, drying herself quickly with a huge towel and wrapping her hair in another.

She had to work out what she was going to do. How she could drag herself out of this impossible situation. Or whether she even wanted to.

Five minutes later the bed was made, pristine, as if it had never been the scene of such a disaster.

A pity her hands were shaking so badly she had to clasp them tight together to stop them shaking. All she wanted to do was curl up and sob herself hoarse.

She straightened her shoulders and walked to the wardrobe. Deliberately she dressed in one of the new outfits Bella had convinced her to buy.

Now, if ever, she needed confidence, and this outfit would give her the boost she needed so desperately. The red fitted dress complemented her curves in a way that made her feel feminine and not, for a change, oversized. The high-standing collar gave way at the front to a neckline that plunged low. She'd seen the way Ronan had looked at her breasts, hot and hungry. The memory sent a thrill of exhilaration through her. She wasn't about to deny herself the chance to make him hunger for them again.

She was sitting on the bed, untangling her wet hair and wishing she could untangle the mess her life had become, when the phone rang.

'Hello?'

'I want to speak to Marina Lucchesi.' Charles Wakefield's unmistakably impatient tone shocked her into silence. 'Can you put her on?'

'It's Marina speaking,' she said, carefully lowering the hair-brush to the bed. What on earth could he want?

She didn't think she could deal with him now. Not when it felt as if her heart was bleeding.

'At last. Charles Wakefield here,' he said, and paused as if waiting for her to respond. 'You've been hiding yourself away, Marina.' His voice was smooth now, playfully chiding, but she picked up a current of anger. 'You haven't returned my PA's calls.'

'Sorry,' she said, frowning. 'What calls?'

Silence.

'My assistant has been ringing you every day. You say you didn't get the messages?'

She shook her head, wondering if she should believe him. 'I haven't had any messages from you.' What was going on? 'Who did he speak to?'

'Does it matter? Whoever it is your lover employs over there.'

Marina sank back against the headboard of the bed, rubbing her temple where a headache had begun. Why would Mrs Sinclair—or Ronan, for that matter—not pass on the messages?

'It sounds like Carlisle doesn't want you to see me,' said the voice on the other end of the line, and Marina had to agree. That was exactly how it sounded.

Mrs Sinclair was too organised to forget messages. She must have been told not to pass them on. But why, when the whole point of Marina being here was supposed to be as a lure to Wakefield?

Her head whirled with a jumble of questions. Nothing made sense. And she couldn't get her mind into gear to work it out.

'I'm sure there's been some mistake,' she offered finally, wondering how she was supposed to play this. She didn't want to deal with Wakefield, but he was the man who held Marina Enterprises, the key to her future and Seb's. And she was supposed to be inviting his interest, not hiding from him.

'Why are you calling?'

'Ah. Now there's a question.' He paused, and she could picture his crocodile smile. She shivered.

'We agreed to meet—don't you recall? Just the two of us. You wanted to discuss Marina Enterprises.'

'That's right.' Her pulse quickened despite her reservations.

'Good. Let's arrange a time to get together. The sooner the better.'

Marina looked up at the sound of her door opening and her breath stalled.

There was Ronan, in faded jeans, open shirt and bare feet, staring back at her across the room. She felt the shock of it deep in her solar plexus. How had she managed to forget how sexy he was? Or that her body thrummed into needy awareness just at the sight of him?

Ashamed, she gripped the phone harder, anchoring herself against the need to forget sanity and plead for more of his lovemaking.

She was a self-destructive idiot. Surely she had more self-respect than that.

'Marina?' Wakefield's voice was sharp. 'I said let's make it soon.'

At last she found her voice. 'I agree…Charles.' She almost grimaced at the sound of his name on her lips. 'As soon as you like.'

Her eyes widened as Ronan strode across the room, tension manifest in every rigid line of his body, his brow folding into a black frown.

'How about tonight?' Wakefield prompted.

Ronan loomed over her now, disapproval clear in his eyes. He stood aggressively close, feet apart and arms akimbo.

She trembled at his aura of barely leashed power. It was too much, too soon. Suddenly she'd have given almost anything for a reprieve before she had to deal with him again. Even if it meant meeting Wakefield.

Tonight? Why not?

'That sounds perfect.' Her voice was husky and she cleared her throat. 'I'll meet you for a drink.' No way was she signing up for a whole evening in Wakefield's company, no matter how desperate she was. 'Where and when?'

She glanced at the bedside clock as he named an expensive bar in the city, realising she'd have to leave soon to make it in time.

'Fine. I'll see you there.' She put down the phone abruptly before she could change her mind. Then she grabbed her brush, began tugging it through her tangled locks.

'You're meeting Wakefield?' Ronan's voice was tight.

'Yes.' She avoided his gaze. 'I just have time to put my make-up on and dry my hair.'

'You're not going to see him now!' He sounded outraged.

'Why not?' She couldn't think when he stood so close—pure invitation to such a needy female. Swallowing down the sour taste of self-knowledge, she pushed to her feet and stepped past him.

Tension pulsed through him, charging the surrounding air and she shivered. 'That was the whole point of this preposterous charade, wasn't it?'

His hand snapped out and clamped around her wrist, pulling her up short. Her senses sang, remembering the magic he'd wrought a mere hour ago. She yearned for his passion and his tenderness.

And that made her furious. How could she be so weak? So self-destructive? To want a man who saw her as no more than a convenient lay and a pawn in a commercial manoeuvre?

She spun round to face him. 'Why didn't anyone tell me his PA has been calling? That he wanted to talk to me?' Her voice rose unsteadily. 'What sort of game are you playing?'

Through the fizz of tension in the air, Ronan felt the inevitable pulse of his driving need thrum into being. Marina's eyes flashed and her body vibrated with indignation. She was totally alluring.

'You needed rest. You've been through a lot recently, and you needed time to recuperate. Letting Wakefield think you were unattainable hasn't done any harm. It's just whetted his interest.'

That was something he didn't want to dwell on. Wakefield had been all but drooling last time he'd clapped eyes on Marina, triggering a violent proprietorial response in Ronan. Wakefield had been lucky to escape that night in one piece.

Ronan watched her eyes narrow as she assessed his logic. Eventually she spoke. 'Well, in future I'd appreciate it if you'd consult me before you interfere.'

He shrugged. 'I've had Wakefield in my sights for so long, I'm used to calling the shots.'

'Not with me, you don't.' Her face was closed, unreadable, except for the angry passion that lit her eyes.

How badly he wanted that passion for himself. Now. Again. Right through the night.

Marina was like a drug in his bloodstream, heating his body to combustible levels.

The only reason he'd forced himself from her bed and into some clothes was the knowledge that it had been her first time. She'd be tender, possibly even sore. And if he'd stayed there, naked against her, nothing would have stopped him taking her again.

'I'll deal with him.' His voice was rough.

'No!' She tugged her hand free and turned away to the open bathroom door. To the wide mirror and the array of cosmetics spread before it. 'I'll meet him. It's my business, after all.'

He scowled.

She was right. It was time she met him. Keeping her incommunicado had served its purpose. Wakefield's interest had reached fever-pitch, judging from the number of calls he'd made. He was the sort who couldn't bear delay—was used to instant gratification.

And while Wakefield had been absorbed in his futile efforts to approach her Ronan had been busy dealing with a few of Wakefield's creditors, as well as acquiring some useful shares.

So why did he revolt at the idea of Marina and Wakefield together? Why did his whole body tense, ready to prevent her leaving?

He heaved in a deep breath and forced his mind to claw back control from his instinct. His eyes skimmed her figure in that clinging red dress, the swathe of her long, inviting hair.

And he felt again the jab of fierce possessiveness.

You can't go tonight because we've just made love and I want you again. Because you were a virgin an hour ago and you need me to cosset you. Because it revolts me to think of you going to meet Wakefield when you're mine. Because he'll take one look at you in that dress and spend the rest of the time imagining you without it.

Because I'm jealous.

He was *jealous*? Of Wakefield?

Impossible.

Wakefield was nothing to Marina but an enemy.

It was *he,* Ronan, who had her in his home, his bed. He'd just initiated her into the secrets of lovemaking and he had the prospect of long, hot nights ahead, expanding on her education.

He was Marina's lover.

Yet there was no denying the unreasoning surge of fury at the idea of Marina spending time with Wakefield. Or with any other man.

What the hell was happening to him? He'd never been a jealous lover. Protective, yes. But this raw possessiveness?

He wiped a hand over his face, as if to scrub away the strange miasma.

'Yes.' He forced himself to nod, to be sensible. 'You'd better see him. But it will have to be a short meeting. I'll get the car out and meet you downstairs.'

Her eyes met his in the bathroom mirror and he almost changed his mind about letting her go. Her glossy lips parted invitingly, and she'd done something to her eyes that accentuated their brilliance. He didn't want her looking like that for anyone except him.

'I'll catch a taxi.'

He shook his head. 'You'll go with me.'

She swung round to face him, skirt flaring around those long, lovely legs. 'Wakefield will think it's odd if you take me to meet him. What lover would do that?'

'Let Wakefield think what he likes. I'm taking you.'

Or you're not going.

She stared at him for the space of two heartbeats, then turned back to the mirror.

He swung round and left the room before he gave in to one of his more primitive urges: to scoop her into his arms, pin her to the bed and keep her there. The way a caveman would react. The way he'd already behaved tonight.

No. Logic dictated that he let Marina and Wakefield meet. And so they would.

All he had to do was find a way to deal with the storm of jealousy that bombarded him at the idea of her going out to meet another man.

CHAPTER FIFTEEN

MARINA pushed her way towards the exit of the trendy bar, ignoring the bustle of activity near the window where Charles Wakefield now sat alone. Except for the waitress mopping up the spill.

A pity he'd ordered a bottle of champagne. Red wine would have left a much more satisfying stain on his silver-grey suit. One that would last.

As she emerged onto the pavement a shadow detached itself from the darkness and fell into step beside her. It was Jackson Bourne, Ronan's chief of security. He'd been detailed to wait, then drive her back. When Ronan had snapped out the order she'd been affronted that he thought she needed a minder. Now she was grateful.

Bourne's large presence reminded her of Ronan. She longed for him. She wanted to throw herself into Ronan's strong arms and rail at the unfairness of it all. Ronan would put his arms around her and tell her it would be all right. That together they'd defeat Wakefield. And that the most important thing to know right now was that he loved her.

Yeah. Right.

Abruptly the righteous indignation that had buoyed her through the scene with Wakefield dissipated. Its loss left her feeling hollow and weak. Her legs trembled and she pulled up abruptly, locking her knees to steady herself.

'Ms Lucchesi? Are you okay?' Bourne's gravelly voice was concerned.

'I'm fine, thanks. Where's the car?' The last thing she needed now was a sympathetic ear. Not if she wanted to get back with her composure still in place.

'Here it is.' He gestured to a gleaming dark sedan.

She got in, watched him pause for a quick conversation on his cellphone before taking the driver's seat. Probably reporting to the boss that he was delivering her back, she thought sourly.

In their different ways Ronan and Wakefield had made her feel like a commodity tonight. Something to be bought and traded and possessed. But she wasn't a chattel, or a prize. She was a woman with her own needs and dreams.

She bit her lip, wishing she could go back now to her own home. She needed the comfort of its safe familiarity. But it had been sold—she had no home.

Marina shivered, recognising the symptoms of exhaustion. She was emotionally vulnerable and her body was tender in places that didn't bear thinking about. Why had she thought she could handle Wakefield tonight of all nights?

Self-pity was tempting. But she couldn't give in to it or she mightn't stop. She bit down hard on her trembling lip and stared out of the window, blinking back tears of defeat and disillusionment.

The car pulled up on the gravel drive before Ronan's home. She opened her door before Bourne switched off the engine.

'Thanks for the lift,' she said over her shoulder as she got out. Her legs were steady now, just leaden with tiredness.

The entrance door opened and Ronan stood there, his broad shoulders and the confident tilt of his head silhouetted against the glowing lights of the vestibule. She checked as a flood of hot, intimate memories surfaced, stealing her breath.

'Marina.'

'Hello, Ronan.' She didn't meet his eyes, and he stepped aside to let her sidle past him into the house.

As she crossed to the stairs, her heels click-clacking on the tiled floor, she heard the murmur of male voices. It crossed her mind to wonder if Bourne had witnessed the scene with Wakefield.

But what did it matter? Half of Sydney could have been there for all she cared.

She'd reached the top of the stairs when Ronan caught up with her.

'Marina.'

'I'm tired, Ronan. I want to go to sleep.'

'We need to talk.' He followed her down the hall.

'Not tonight.' She was too keyed-up to sleep, but she craved solitude. She didn't have the strength to maintain this crumbling façade of independence much longer. She just wanted to lock herself in her room and sob her eyes out in the welcoming darkness.

'Have you eaten?'

'I'm not hungry,' she said, her attention on her bedroom door a few rooms away. Sanctuary.

'Good,' he said, and she felt his hand, large and uncompromising, shackle her wrist. 'Then you won't mind if we talk rather than eat.' He drew her towards his own bedroom, shoving the door open with his other hand.

'No!' She jerked back, desperate to break his grasp.

'Yes,' he said, pulling her inexorably into his private space. 'Don't worry, I'm not going to bite you.'

But Marina had had enough of managing, manipulative men tonight. She squirmed, pulling with all her might, trying to inch her way back into the hall. 'Let me go!'

'Damn it, Marina, I need to talk to you.'

She was past caring. Past hearing. She'd finally reached breaking point. Her struggles grew wilder, her breathing shallow as she fought to break his hold.

And suddenly it was over. With one powerful movement he swung them both round and she was trapped, her back flush with the wall. Ronan pressed his hard body against her from breast to knee. His hands splayed flat on the wall at either side of her head.

She couldn't get enough purchase to move. Could barely gasp for the air she needed with his chest weighting hers. She was surrounded, helpless.

But despite her impotent fury an insidious curl of desire unfurled and spread through her body. It drew her skin tight and made her mind race.

Being jammed up against his hard body was intoxicating. Suffocating. Tension pulsed between them, a palpable force.

She sagged, her body surrendering to the overwhelming power of her emotions.

How had she ever found the strength to walk out on him this evening? To turn her back and meet Wakefield? It wasn't simply that Ronan dominated her with his physical superiority. It was her heart, her own longings, that held her in thrall to Ronan Carlisle. She didn't have the strength left to fight that any more.

He didn't love her, didn't need her. But she loved and needed enough for the two of them. Her pride was dust.

'Marina.' His voice was a husky whisper across her temple and she raised her face, deluding herself that she heard longing in that single word.

She licked her parched lips, knowing she should say something, anything, to shatter the intimacy that threatened to destroy the shreds of her self-control.

And then, so abruptly she almost slid on useless legs down the wall, he stepped back, allowing her freedom. Her soul cried out in torment, bereft without him.

For a silent moment he stood, watching her. She felt the touch of his gaze but she wouldn't meet his eyes.

She blinked as his hand enfolded hers and he led her across the room. She didn't even protest when he pulled her down to sit beside him on the huge bed. Her brain had atrophied, overloaded by a tide of emotional turmoil. She felt numb.

He cradled her hand in his palm and she watched, fascinated, as he covered it with his other hand. His thumb rubbed slowly, rhythmically, over her wrist, sending quivers through her body.

'Marina.' She could read nothing in his voice except soothing reassurance. 'What happened when you saw Wakefield?'

She felt a flicker of emotion burn, then fade. Disappointment. He really did want to talk.

Surely she hadn't thought he'd want to make love with her again? Once had clearly been enough for him. Where were her wits? Her self-respect?

She stared at his hands: large, capable and well-shaped. Against his sinewed strength her own hand looked delicate.

'Marina,' he urged softly. 'What happened?'

She frowned, swallowing down the bile that rose in her throat. She could see Wakefield now, suave and elegant with his custom-made suit and solarium tan. And his sly innuendo.

Ronan raised a hand to her jaw and tilted her head so he could see her face. His own was unreadable but for the tension he couldn't hide.

'Well? Are you going to tell me?'

And that was when she recognised it. Impatience. And more than that. Concern. He was worried for her.

She watched the muscles in his jaw shift and clench. The pulse in his neck grew more pronounced. And she knew beyond a shadow of doubt that Ronan would inflict savage retribution on Wakefield. There was suppressed violence in his rigid stillness. All it would take was a word from her to unleash it. Wakefield was his sworn enemy.

She pictured herself giving him the excuse he wanted. Telling him Wakefield had been interested, but he hadn't bothered to exert his fabled charm on her. Oh, no. He'd taken particular delight in being crudely forthright about what she had to do to make him rethink his ownership of Marina Enterprises. Dump Ronan and become his own 'special friend'.

She'd known Wakefield was scum. Tonight had merely confirmed it. His filthy suggestion was only what she should have expected from the man who'd cheated her brother so ruthlessly.

She felt unclean at the memory of Wakefield's insult, of his leer and his hungry smile. And she knew Ronan's response to her revelation would be swift and violent. He'd probably end up on an assault charge.

Wakefield wasn't worth that.

'If he's hurt you I'll destroy him.' His fingers stiffened against her chin. 'Right now.' Ronan's voice was a savage rumble. She knew instinctively he meant what he said.

'No!' She lifted her hand to clasp his strong wrist, and felt the pulse thud roughly under his hot skin.

'No. There's nothing to get worked up about.' She stared straight back into his electric gaze, willing him to believe her. 'He was interested, but non-committal,' she lied. 'I just don't like being alone with him.' That much at least was true. 'He gives me the creeps.'

Ronan's scrutiny was so intense she felt it slide across her heated skin. She managed to hold his gaze until he lifted his hand and rubbed his thumb over the frown creasing her brow. Such a gentle caress, so intimate.

'He didn't try to touch you?'

'No.' He'd expected her to make all the moves instead.

'You won't be alone with him again.'

She swallowed hard at the sound of his low-voiced pledge and acknowledged the seductive desire to let Ronan shoulder her burden. She'd never let anyone fight her battles in the past. No one had offered. But now he was assuming that right. And, Lord help her, she couldn't find it in her to argue any longer.

He didn't love her, but he'd protect her from Wakefield.

'I should never have let you see him alone.' Fury vibrated in his voice. 'In future I'll deal with him. No matter what he promises, you keep away from him.'

She nodded, glad to be on safe ground. 'I will.'

'You trust me to take care of everything?' he murmured. His hand stroked from her brow to her cheek, sending thrills of delight through her, making a mockery of her attempt to control her responses. She lifted her eyes to his.

She had no qualms now about leaving everything in Ronan's hands. If anyone could retrieve Marina Enterprises, he could. He had the power and the business savvy. And his protectiveness showed he had her interests at heart, if only because he felt sorry for her. He'd do what he could for her and Seb.

'I— Yes. Yes, I do.' It was a relief to admit it.

Heat flared in his eyes. Her breath snagged at the intensity of his gaze. His hand cupped her cheek and he brushed his thumb across her lips once, twice, parting them with gentle pressure. Her mouth tingled and she fought the desperate urge to sway closer to him. To press her aching, sensitive nipples against the wall of his chest and invite him to take her again.

She needed to leave. Before she was lost. She shut her eyes, trying to summon the strength to move away. But the darkness only intensified the intimacy of his touch, the overwhelming surge of longing that weakened her body and her resolve.

When she opened her eyes his face was closer, and a shiver of urgent expectancy raced up her spine.

'I should go now,' she whispered. Even to her own ears she didn't sound convincing. Where was her willpower? Hadn't she decided he was too dangerous for her peace of mind?

He lifted his other hand to smooth up her bare arm, sending shivers of awareness over her flesh as he caressed her shoulder, then brushed the nape of her neck. Her breath hissed out as he tunnelled his fingers through her hair, massaging her scalp in slow, sensuous circles that liquefied her bones.

'Ronan. I really think…' Her words petered out as he leaned close and touched his lips to the corner of her mouth. It was a tiny, barely-there kiss. And it ignited an explosion of desperate need in her. Her recently awakened body responded with voracious hunger to the memory of ecstasy. Ecstasy wrought so easily and so devastatingly by this man.

He drew away just enough to look into her eyes and his hands stilled. He held her, but a single movement would break his hold. She could leave him now if she wanted to.

She should be relieved. Instead she was confused, appalled by her own lack of resolve.

He was giving her a choice. She read the question in his expression, the controlled energy in his bunched muscles.

She *should* leave him. Now. While she could still think. She'd invite heartbreak if she let him make love to her again. Such intimacy could only bind her closer.

After just one time the sensations were scorched into her brain. His erotic caresses, the slide of his body against hers, his ragged hot breath in her ear, his shuddering climax, the raw power of him thrusting inside her: every memory was addictive.

Her chest heaved with her rapid, uneven breathing as the now-familiar need pulsed through her, shattering the last of her control.

This man excited her. More than that, he held her heart.

How could she deny herself when he was everything she wanted?

Tentatively she reached out and touched him, her trembling palm flat against the cotton of his shirt. Beneath her fingers thudded a heartbeat as rapid as her own. It throbbed, vibrating against his powerful chest, testimony to his desire for her.

That shouldn't make a difference. If she knew what was good for her she'd get out of here now.

But inevitably it made all the difference in the world. He cared for her. Unlike his rival, who merely saw her as a tool to be used in a crude power contest. Ronan felt something for her, even if it wasn't love. And in this moment he desired her.

Her, Marina Lucchesi. Big, buxom, scarred Marina. The woman who'd fallen headlong into love with him.

She didn't have a hope of letting her head rule her heart. Especially when he chose that moment to spell out his intentions.

'I want to make love with you, Marina. Properly this time. I want to show you just how good it can be between us.' His low voice was a husky burr that alone was enough to seduce. 'You deserve more than I gave you before. Much more.'

Heat washed her cheeks and she shivered helplessly, knowing she was lost. She barely registered the rest of his words. It was the raw desire in his fever-bright eyes, the urgency of his hungry growl, that she understood.

Gaze still locked with hers, he took her hand, raised it to his mouth and centred a slow, erotic kiss on her palm. She felt his tongue flick across that sensitive point and a riot of sensation burst through her body. It heated the very core of her. Need was a potent, writhing force consuming her. She had no defence against it.

His eyes told her he was waiting for her response. Her shuddering delight at his caress wasn't enough.

She slid her palm up his chest to the radiant heat of his bare neck. His muscles strained with tension, but he sat rigidly still as her fingers spread up through his hair. It was marvellously soft and sexy on such a hard, masculine man.

She watched him swallow convulsively and registered the finest of tremors in his long fingers.

He leaned close, till his face was bare centimetres from hers, till his hot breath seared her skin. Deliberately, unhurriedly, he kissed her full on the mouth, and she thrilled to the way his strong arms gathered her close. They lashed around her needily, protectively. And she responded, melting against him like wax before a flame.

He was all strength and power and tenderness. A fantasy come to life.

Slowly, with intense deliberation, he laid her on the bed and stripped her clothes away. She lay pliant beneath his sure touch, her breath arrested at the promise of ecstasy to come. His burning gaze held her still, dazed by the enormity of her emotions.

And then it was impossible to lie passive any more. He'd dispensed with her clothes, and now his fingers skimmed, stroked, teased and excited. He caressed her so sensuously, making her quiver with delight and longing.

Finally he lowered his head and kissed her again.

Desire. Love. They welled up inside her. She thought she'd explode then and there at the perfection of the moment as she felt his lips slide against hers, his tongue delve into her mouth, his hot breath mingle with hers. His weight upon her, as she pulled him close, stimulated a wild yearning.

But there was more.

When he took her nipple in his mouth, first delicately laving and then suckling hard, she sobbed with relief. She was wound up too tight, the tension building in her till she thought something would break if he didn't love her soon. She was desperate for him, her hands skimming restlessly, urging him close.

Yet he refused to rush. He moved on, exploring, nuzzling and kissing and smoothing his hands in the lightest of caresses, all over her. Over her shoulders, down her hips and calves, to the arches of her feet, and back up along her inner thighs to the place between her legs where the fire blazed brightest. Liquid heat seared her veins and pooled low in anticipation.

She throbbed with unfulfilled need as she twisted beneath his ministrations, eager for so much more. But he used his strength to overpower her frantic attempts to undress him. His hands clamped her wrists. His heavy thigh restrained her legs. His solid weight pushed her down against the mattress.

He heaped sensation after amazing sensation on her, denying her the fulfilment of his own body. Hoarse gasps filled her ears and whimpering mews of need. The sound of her falling apart, mindless with wanting him.

He slid low, licked from her waist to her ribcage. She shuddered and slipped her hands from his hold. Blindly she scrabbled at his shirt, popping buttons in her haste.

One large hand captured both of hers, pressing them to his chest, curbing her frenzied movements. And then he met her eyes. She sucked in her breath in shock. His eyes scorched so hot that they should have burnt her to cinders. His face was a tight mask, almost of pain, that told its own story of the immense self-control he was exerting.

'Ronan.' She swallowed hard, her throat parched, raw with desperation. 'Let me!'

He shook his head and lowered his mouth to her breast.

'Ronan, please!'

He stopped, his mouth a breath away from her nipple. Then he lifted his head and held himself above her. His storm-dark gaze probed, as if testing the truth of her words. He looked grim, utterly unyielding.

'I *need* you.'

Something flickered in his expression, and suddenly she was free. Ronan rolled away, ripped his clothes off in savage haste. Her breath caught at the sight of his body. Beautiful. Rampant. Hers.

He reached for protection and then he returned. But now his movements were careful. His deliberation belied his haste a moment before. But the way he trembled told her just how much it cost him to move slowly.

He lowered himself to lie over her, trapping her in a world that began and ended with his strong, gorgeous body. She loved the feel of him. The scratch of his hairy legs against hers. The erotic sensation of his torso, solid and lightly covered in hair, heaving against her breasts. The weight of him pressed hard against her abdomen, inciting a fever of shuddering desire.

She wanted all of him, every glorious inch of his magnificent body. And she wanted him now.

She almost cried with relief when he spread her thighs and braced himself, poised above her. His sex nudged her, tested, and then slowly, with the inexorable power of a swelling tide, he entered, stretching her taut muscles. Her eyes widened. He filled her further and further, till surely any more was impossible.

'Lift your knees,' he whispered.

Tentatively she obeyed, felt a momentary relief of the pressure, and then gasped as he slid right to her core, coming to rest deep within her.

Had it been this impossibly magnificent before? She was anchored to him, part of him, whole.

She tilted her hips up a fraction, amazed at the feel of them together.

'No!' His voice was hoarse. 'Don't move,' he gasped.

He propped himself above her on arms taut with strain. His mouth was a line of pain, and every clenched muscle in his hard body spoke of iron-willed control. Sweat budded on his brow and at the base of his throat.

But Marina was greedy for more. He smelt musky and sensual, inviting. She lifted her head and licked his neck, taking the salt tang, the pure essence of Ronan, into her mouth.

He groaned and shuddered.

She wrapped her arms around him, hugging him to her, knowing that she never wanted to let him go.

'Yes,' she said, tilting her hips provocatively, revelling in the surge of sensation where their bodies joined.

For a moment his control held, and then, with a whoosh of hot air, he expelled the breath he'd been holding and metamorphosed from human statue into pure energy. He took control, moving swiftly, expertly, in a primitive rhythm she instinctively matched. Faster and harder and stronger.

Marina clutched at him, holding tight, as if she could contain the erotic energy that pulsed through him. It frightened as much as it exhilarated. But then it erupted into her body—a storm unleashed. Sparking heat like lightning flashed through her, blinding her, electrifying her senses. She juddered, the shocking intensity of power too strong for her. The world spun and she cried out in pleasure so fierce she thought she'd die.

Fulfilment crashed upon them both: long, bone-jarringly intense and utterly wonderful.

Through a haze of sensation she felt him pulse hard within her, heard his rough groan of release against her hair just as she started floating back to earth, his name still on her lips and ringing in her ears.

CHAPTER SIXTEEN

SHE was trapped, unable to move on with her life. But not because of Wakefield's takeover, or Ronan's plans to wrest her company back.

Her priorities had changed.

Marina stared across the flagstones to the brilliant azure of the pool. Yet it was Ronan she saw in her mind's eye.

With his relentless energy, his passion and tenderness, he had taken up residence in her heart. He was the strongest, most fascinating man she'd ever met. He made her feel like a new woman and she loved it.

She told herself he didn't need her, didn't really need her. But the knowledge made no difference to her feelings. She craved him. As a lover, a partner, the other half of herself.

For now it was almost enough to be desired. Even with her rounded body and her smart mouth and her scars—all the things she'd believed would keep any man away. But not Ronan. A spasm of excitement lanced through her when she remembered his hot wanting looks, as if he couldn't get enough of her. He desired her so blatantly that she felt powerful—confident and sexy as never before.

Even now, away on urgent business, Ronan made her feel special. He rang daily, and the sound of his voice, husky with intimate shared memories, made her blood race and her body come alive. The calls came from Tokyo, Beijing and Perth. They made her realise how pathetically she loved him, when the high point of her day was the sound of his voice from thousands of kilometres away.

To make it worse, she felt guilty about lying. She hadn't admitted she was there under false pretences. Her value to Ronan's plan had vanished as soon as she'd reacted to Wakefield's suggestion that she prostitute herself for Marina Enterprises. Wakefield wouldn't chase a virago. Yet she hadn't told Ronan about that incident. If she did she'd have no reason to stay. Her part in his scheme would be over.

She had no illusions. Ronan cared for her, desired her, and pursued their affair with a voracious appetite. But he'd never mentioned permanency. This was a fling. Sooner or later his passion would burn out.

Despite the afternoon sun she felt a bone-deep chill.

Marina stared past the glittering pool, dreading the decision she had to make. The specialist had told her this morning that her recovery had been excellent. She could return to work soon, part-time. She should be pleased.

That was what she needed: to focus on her future. She'd strived hard to get her accounting qualifications, had worked just as hard for the company, and had thrived on the knowledge that she was darned good at what she did. She still had a job, even though the transfer was complete and Wakefield now owned Marina Enterprises. He hadn't sacked her—yet. She could work there while she found another position.

Then she'd need somewhere to live.

She swallowed the sour taste of reality and forced her mind to the future. A future that didn't include Ronan. She ached at the idea of leaving him. But eventually he'd want her to go. Better she went with dignity and had her departure planned. She couldn't risk him finding out how badly she wanted to stay.

She'd had enough of being an object of pity.

Reluctantly she reached for the newspaper on the patio table before her. She'd already circled some flats to let. She should ring about them, but the action seemed so final, like the end of a dream, that she couldn't do it.

Abruptly she pushed her chair back, strode to the pool-edge

and dived in. The silken water closed round her, cool against her tense muscles. Maybe if she pushed herself hard enough the pain would go away.

When she stopped, gulping air and blinking water from her eyes, her breath jammed in her throat as she saw Ronan. It was as if she'd conjured him from her troubled thoughts.

Lovingly she scanned his powerful body. He wore only swimmers, a towel slung over his shoulder. Her pulse quickened, excitement filling her. What was he doing back two days early?

She watched the play of muscles across his back as he threw his towel down beside hers. He was like a sun god, bathed in the golden light of late afternoon. His perfect physique utterly masculine.

Trembling awareness weakened her limbs; the heavy coil of desire began to spiral within her. Would she ever break this spell he had over her?

He turned and she saw his frown, unmistakable strain evident in his fisted hands. Her own brows creased and she wondered what was wrong as she swam towards him.

She'd only done a couple of strokes when she felt his powerful slipstream as he turned in the water beneath her. A pair of strong hands fastened on her ribs, pulling her up. She surfaced in his arms and couldn't prevent a smile as she tilted her head up towards his.

'Hello, Ronan.'

'Marina.' His voice was deep and mesmerising, just as she'd remembered it in her dreams each night. And then he was kissing her, pulling her hard against him in a display of power that was as unnecessary as it was wonderful.

She felt her heart tumble over in her chest. How she loved him. How would she cope when she had to leave him?

When he broke the kiss he kept his arms around her. She clung to him, loving the sensation of his body pressed against hers. All that refined power, that tensile strength so close and so tempting.

'What's wrong?' she asked, seeing the grim line of his mouth.

'You're looking at flats to let?' His voice was harsh, accusing.

It was the last thing she'd expected him to say, and she hesitated, uneasy, as if she'd been caught out at something. 'I was just checking what's available.'

His arms tightened round her, but he didn't say anything. She could feel the tension in his rigid muscles and in the rapid thud of his heart against her chest.

Was he angry that she was showing some of her old independence? That must mean he wasn't yet ready to end their liaison. That he still wanted her. A thrill of excitement curled through her at the knowledge. It was quashed seconds later by the chill voice of common sense, warning her she'd be an emotional wreck if she waited for him to end the affair, as he inevitably would.

'I need to think about the future.' She watched him intently, foolishly wishing he'd interrupt and declare her future was with him. Of course he didn't.

'I went to the doctor today.'

A flash of potent emotion appeared in his eyes, lighting the indigo depths with blazing heat. But it was gone before she could put a name to it.

'What did he say?' Ronan's voice was clipped, almost as if he'd braced himself for news.

Marina wondered if she'd grown fanciful, reading significance into a simple question. His face was enigmatic, no emotion at all.

'He said I've made a terrific recovery.' She forced her lips into a smile, knowing she should be ecstatic at the news instead of feeling that her heart would break. 'He says I can go back to work soon. Just a few hours a day to start with. Isn't that wonderful?'

'Wonderful.' His tone was expressionless, as was his shuttered face. She frowned. She didn't know what she'd expected from him, but this grim watchfulness wasn't it.

'You want to return to work?'

She nodded slowly.

'And you want to find a place to live?'

'Well, I… Yes. Yes, I do,' she lied, over the sound of her giddy dreams of love crashing around her. This was so much easier than she'd expected. Much easier than she wanted it to be. She schooled her features to match her calm tone. He'd never guess how hard this was for her.

'Your plans will just have to wait.' His face was all harsh lines, and his eyes flashed fire as his arms stiffened around her.

'I don't understand. Why should they wait?'

For a long moment he stared at her, almost as if stumped by her question.

'We haven't finished with Wakefield—or had you forgotten? I need you here with me till that's finished.' He paused. 'You don't want to jeopardise our chance of making him pay for what he's done.'

'I'd be happy just to get Marina Enterprises back,' she said. 'But me being here won't make any difference.'

'You think not?' His eyes glinted. 'Then you have no idea how valuable a diversion you've already been. He hasn't been alert enough to the warning signs in his own companies.'

Now was the time to tell him the truth—that Wakefield was no longer interested in her. 'It won't make any difference—'

'And there's another reason you need to stay.' He lowered his head till his mouth was a breath away from hers. She swallowed hard, trying to ignore the burgeoning need as his voice turned low and harsh. Forbidden excitement swirled deep inside her.

'There is?'

'Yes.' He nodded, his eyes never leaving hers. 'This.'

Water rippled around them as he pushed her against the tiled wall of the pool. She was out of her depth and grabbed his shoulders for support, though she wouldn't have sunk. His body was jammed against hers, trapping her.

Then she stopped thinking as he kissed her. It was unlike anything they'd shared before, even their urgent, almost angry passion the first time he'd loved her.

It was compelling, fired by a frantic hunger and fuelled by his recent absence. He plundered her mouth with a marauder's kiss, hot and urgent and breathtaking. She wanted all that and more, revelling in his fierce need, meeting his desire with her own. He surged against her as if he couldn't get close enough, his hands heavy and hot on her slick skin.

He felt so good. So right. Even better than she remembered. How could anything so wonderful be so destructive?

'I missed you,' he murmured against her lips, and even that

was enough to make her heart sing. 'And you missed me,' he said, as he stroked the tender flesh behind her ear with his tongue.

'Didn't you?' he demanded.

'Yes,' she whispered as she clung to him. 'I missed you, Ronan.'

He nipped at her earlobe and she shivered, knowing that she didn't have the strength to leave him. Not yet. Not when he kissed her like this, wanted her like this.

It was only the roughness of his hands on her swimsuit that brought her back to realisation of their surroundings. He pushed her arms off his shoulders and tugged at her shoulder straps, sliding them down.

'Ronan! We can't. Not here.' She peered over his shoulder towards the house.

'Of course we can.' He palmed her now bare breasts and squeezed. Darts of hot sensation speared her, arrowing down to the place where he pushed, hard and ready, between her legs. She gasped and tried to control the shudder that rippled through her. The desire burning within, the loosening of all her muscles ready for lovemaking.

And he could see it all, damn him. The knowing gleam of satisfaction was there in his eyes.

'Mrs Sinclair…' she began, fighting for control.

He shook his head and rubbed her nipples between his fingers, making her gasp. 'I gave her the rest of the day off.' His look was pure predator. 'We're all alone. No one can see us. The gates are locked. There'll be no intruders.'

Marina felt him pulse against her and gave up the fight. She didn't know how much longer she had left with him. But she wasn't masochistic enough to deny his passion while she had it. It made her feel dizzy, reckless with desire and love.

'Good.' She shoved at his broad chest.

He backed a scant few centimetres and she thrust his hands away. She was beyond thought when he touched her like that. Then, with a single sinuous movement, she slid her swimsuit down past her waist, over her hips and thighs, submerging to bend and kick the Lycra off her legs.

She had a perfect view of Ronan's legs, planted wide apart,

of his erection straining against the fabric of his swimmers. She reached out to snag her fingers over his waistband.

There was a flurry of movement as he grabbed her wrist and hauled her to the surface. Before she could protest he pushed her up against the tiles again. Her breath expelled in a single whoosh of surprise and thrilled expectation. One large hand pulled her thigh up and round his waist as the other disposed of his swimmers.

She closed her eyes in relief at the feel of him against her. This was what she wanted so badly. It was like fire in the blood, blazing stronger all the time. He lifted her other leg, wrapping it round him, and she pulled herself up so that her nipples brushed the firm contours of his chest. She shuddered at the erotic friction.

'Yes,' he urged, his voice thick. 'Higher.' Then, with one abrupt, decisive movement, he pushed up into her.

Her eyes snapped open to meet his as the tremors started.

'Yes,' he said again, and the tenderness she read in his eyes filled her heart with answering emotion.

'Hold on.' His face clenched into a mask of concentration as passion took over. She clung to him as he thrust harder and faster, and the world began to spiral out of control in the most wonderful way.

Still his eyes held hers, till she could hold back no longer and she shouted his name in her ecstasy, needing him, loving him.

As if it was the signal he'd been waiting for, Ronan thrust one last time, gathering her up against him, and buried his face in her neck as shudder after shudder thundered through him.

Marina wrapped her arms around him, feeling the most ridiculous urge to protect him. This big, strong man who held her life and her happiness in his hands.

She shut her eyes, wondering how she could find a way to fight against love.

Ronan straightened his tie as he looked down at Marina, sleeping in his bed. She was curled up right in the middle. Exactly where she'd lain with her head on his shoulder till he'd forced himself to move. She hadn't even stirred when he slid out from the bed.

Hell, he was exhausted too. After breaking all records to get two weeks' work completed in barely five days, and after the long flight back from Perth, he'd spent the whole night making love to Marina.

And he wanted to rip the suit off right now and resume what they'd been doing as the first dawn light had crept into the room.

But he couldn't do it. Not today. He had one last item to finalise in the office before he took a well-deserved break.

He had everything organised.

He scowled, remembering the surprise that had greeted him yesterday. The news that Marina was planning to leave had stopped him in his tracks. How ironic that she planned to go now, just when all his efforts had come together and his hostile takeover of several Wakefield enterprises was complete.

And the fact that she'd been to visit a doctor had stunned him.

Instantly his mind had filled with an image of Marina turning to him with her sultry smile and saying she was pregnant. That she was going to have their child.

Even now the idea tripped his pulse, caught his breath in his throat.

Marina, swollen with *his* child.

He'd never thought about having kids before. It had always been part of some nebulous future. He'd never been envious of his mates who'd settled down to marriage and family life.

But now… The intensity of his excitement shocked him.

His hands fisted as that hot, possessive hunger took hold of him again. With Marina he was a man driven by his most primitive instincts. They overrode logic, even his careful plans.

The situation was out of control.

But he knew exactly what he was going to do about it.

CHAPTER SEVENTEEN

'MS LUCCHESI? There's a call for you.'

Marina looked up from her breakfast.

Mrs Sinclair frowned as she held out the cellphone. 'It's Mr Wakefield.' Her carefully controlled voice told Marina the older woman's opinion of him matched her own.

She shivered. It was like being told the serpent had arrived in the Garden of Eden. Which was stupid. Wakefield couldn't hurt her now. Ronan had promised he'd see to it, and she knew he would.

'Thanks.' She nodded to the housekeeper and made herself reach for the phone.

'Marina Lucchesi,' she said at last, pushing away her plate and sitting back in her chair.

'About time,' Wakefield said in her ear. 'I've got some papers for you. We need to meet.'

And hello to you too. He had to be the rudest man she'd ever met. But if he thought he could make her jump at his bidding he was mistaken. She wasn't meeting him again. Once had been enough.

'I'm sorry, Mr Wakefield, we no longer have any business to discuss.'

'That's just where you're wrong, sweetheart.' His honeyed tone barely concealed some strong emotion that made the skin at the back of her neck prickle. 'This is your business. Yours and your brother's. I've got the transfer documents for Marina Enterprises with me.'

Marina froze in her chair. It couldn't be. Could it?

She knew Ronan's plans were progressing. But surely he'd have told her if they were this close to victory?

'Did you hear me?' Wakefield barked in her ear. He certainly didn't sound like a man on a winning streak.

'I heard.'

'Good. Get them to open the security gates. I'm a couple of blocks away. I'll be there in a few minutes.'

Let him in here? The idea appalled her. And she'd told Ronan she wouldn't meet Wakefield alone again.

But how could she refuse? If he was here, ready to sign back the company, could she risk turning him away? Who knew what devious scheme he might find to keep control of it after all?

'Or aren't you interested any more?' the detestable, silky voice taunted, as if confirming her fears.

Marina straightened her shoulders. 'I'll have the gates opened for you,' she said, and took a savage delight in ending the call before he could.

She didn't want to see him again. Her skin crawled at the thought. How she wished Ronan were here, instead of closeted in some high-priority meeting. Mrs Sinclair had said he'd be tied up all morning. And she had no chance of getting her lawyer here so quickly.

She'd have to deal with him herself.

Charles Wakefield still looked brashly successful, she decided ten minutes later, as they faced each other over a coffee table in the sitting room. He was the picture of sophisticated prosperity, with his Italian suit, glossy shoes and whiter than white teeth. Yet he'd changed since she'd last seen him.

This close, she saw how the frown lines were carved deeper on his forehead. The pouches under his eyes bulged more prominently. His deep bronze tan couldn't conceal those signs of strain, or the pinched tightness of his thin lips.

He wasn't the same smug powerbroker he'd been only weeks before.

His eyes flicked over her, assessing, like a bidder in a sale yard, and she stiffened. She stared straight back and watched with satisfaction as his eyes narrowed and he shifted in his seat.

'Your friend Ronan has been busy. I congratulate him.' His sarcasm gave the lie to his words. 'It's obvious he's had quite an incentive.' Again his gaze skimmed her, in a leer that undressed her as she sat.

'What do you want?' she demanded, ignoring the heat flooding her cheeks.

He smiled at her obvious discomfort. 'I told you. I've got those papers you wanted.' He leaned forward. 'You do still want them, don't you, Marina?'

She nodded.

Slowly, eyes still on her, he opened his attaché case and drew out a wad of documents. He glanced down, his smirk transforming into a frown as he scanned the cover sheet.

'The papers transferring my ownership of Marina Enterprises,' he said slowly. 'Just how much are they worth to you?' Abruptly he lifted his head, spearing her with his hungry gaze. 'Enough to give me what I want? To give me what you've been giving Carlisle these past weeks?'

Nausea welled in her throat. So that was why he'd come to see her rather than let the lawyers finalise everything. He just didn't give up.

'You've already had my answer on that.' She surged to her feet. 'This is about my business, not my body!'

'I thought so.' Wakefield grinned at her, leaning back in his seat. 'You really do believe it, don't you?'

'Believe what?' she snapped.

'Such innocence,' he mocked, shaking his head. 'And such a waste. You've obviously fallen in love with Carlisle. Which means you won't get to find out how superior I am to him in so many ways. Especially in bed.'

Bile rose in her throat, almost choking her. 'Get out of here. Now!'

But he merely smiled back at her. 'Such a waste,' he murmured again.

That was it. Marina marched across the room. She'd have no

hope of ejecting Wakefield if he refused to shift, but Ronan's security staff would see to it.

'If you leave now you won't get the papers I've brought you,' he taunted. 'They're already signed.'

Signed? She paused. If they were already signed then it was all over. Warily Marina turned to face him. He shuffled the documents on his knee, then slapped them down on the coffee table.

'There,' he said, in that smooth voice she didn't trust. 'Signed and delivered.' Then he sat back in his chair, arms stretched out over the upholstery.

Marina frowned. It had to be a trick. But she was already heading back, compelled to find out what was going on. He made no move to stop her picking them up. She walked round the coffee table and sank onto the sofa.

'This isn't for Marina Enterprises,' she said, after a moment's perusal of the top sheets. 'It's a copy of the documents for the sale of my house.' She sent him a curious glance, but Wakefield only shrugged.

She flicked through the contract and stopped at the next document. Company records this time, for Australis Holdings. She knew that name. Quickly she referred to the sale contract. Her house had been sold to Australis Holdings. She'd assumed it was a family trust.

Then, rapidly scanning the pages, she found what he wanted her to see. Her pulse stalled for a second before the blood rushed in her ears, the buzzing so loud she could barely hear Wakefield when he spoke again.

'Our friend Carlisle couldn't wait for you to come to him, could he? The sale to one of his companies was rushed through. Leaving you homeless. And vulnerable.'

Marina ignored him, frantically double-checking the papers in her trembling hands.

But it was true. Ronan *had* bought her home, insisting on an immediate settlement at the same time as he'd demanded that she move in here.

Her forehead puckered. He'd pretended he hadn't known about the sale. What had he to gain by doing this?

She delved further and came to the final document, sinking back wide-eyed as she read it.

According to this, Charles Wakefield had transferred ownership of Marina Enterprises two days ago. But the name Lucchesi appeared nowhere on the document. Instead, the new owner was Ronan Carlisle.

CHAPTER EIGHTEEN

PAIN sliced through Marina, so sharp and raw it held her motionless, afraid even to breathe. It stabbed deep, so real she could have sworn she felt bleeding inside.

Last night, as she'd lain in Ronan's arms, he'd already been the owner of her family firm.

The invisible knife twisted savagely.

He'd known then. He must have known. But he hadn't said anything.

Her body chilled to numbness as foreboding swept through her. If he'd known, why hadn't he told her?

'It's painful having one's illusions shattered.' The spurious sympathy in Wakefield's voice didn't have the power to annoy her now. She was too busy trying to grasp the meaning of the agreement before her. Yet she heard every word he said.

'I don't know what line Carlisle fed you,' he was saying, 'but he was out for his own gain. He'd had his eye on your little company for some time. My staff found out about his interest, so I decided to get it first.'

She looked up to see him watching her closely.

'I should have been more cautious,' he admitted with a casual shrug. 'I've made a few…unorthodox acquisitions lately that have become troublesome. Given Carlisle's continuing interest, I've sold this particular one to him. That's what he wanted all along.'

He shook his head and flashed his crocodile smile at her. She shuddered, helpless in the grip of dread.

'You thought *I* was greedy, sweetheart. But at least I was up-front. Carlisle wanted you *and* the company, but he didn't tell you that, did he? He scammed you into thinking he'd help you win back what you'd lost, when all the time he wanted it for himself. He was after the company and a bit of variety in his bed.'

His words sank into silence. Frantically she read and reread the pages. They spilled to her lap from nerveless fingers.

It couldn't be. She knew Ronan didn't love her. But he was a decent man. She'd trusted him.

'One last thing.' Through her blurred vision she saw Wakefield stand. 'Once your precious Ronan knows you've discovered what he's done, your tenure here will be over. He won't want you around, sulking about how he did you wrong.' He paused, then spoke again from the doorway.

'My advice is to get out before he throws you out. You may be decorative, but anyone can see you're not his usual type. I guarantee your novelty value has worn off now. If you have any pride left, you'll leave here instead of waiting to be chucked out.'

The words sank in, but Marina didn't respond, didn't move. There was a rushing, swirling sensation in her head, making her giddy, sucking the air from her lungs in shallow, desperate breaths.

It couldn't be. It couldn't. Not Ronan.

He'd cared for her. Hadn't he?

Tears swam in her eyes and she squeezed them shut. Had it all been a sham?

Ronan had wanted her, all right. He'd needed her to help with his scheme to strip Wakefield of his assets. There was no doubting the intensity of his fury as he'd spoken of what had happened to his sister, or his hatred for Wakefield.

But had he also been motivated by the desire to help Marina? Or had she been only a convenient dupe? After all, she'd never got round to asking for an agreement in writing that he'd pass the company over to her.

She'd been so gullible. So trusting. Even after what had happened to Seb. She should have known the Lucchesi family was out of its depth among the rich and powerful.

Her chest ached with a burning intensity as she fought to keep the tears at bay. It was a fruitless exercise. She felt them, hot and bitter, running down her cheeks and chin.

Ronan owed her no loyalty.

Could it be true? The question circled again and again in her shocked brain.

A novelty, Wakefield had said. Was that how Ronan had seen her? Had his passion, his wonderful, smoking-hot desire, merely been enthusiasm for something new? She wouldn't have thought it of Ronan, would have said it was impossible.

If it weren't for the papers Wakefield had left behind.

She swayed as another blast of pain rocked her. Had that been it? Had her makeover been some sort of sick joke?

She gasped and bent double, arms wrapped tight round her, as if she could stop the agony from welling inside her. Had Ronan been laughing at her all the time? Had he enjoyed taking the ugly duckling and pretending he had transformed it into a swan?

He couldn't be so cruel.

She'd never quite believed his compliments on how beautiful she looked. They'd been designed to boost her confidence; she knew that. But she'd hoped, had secretly clung to the idea, that she'd transformed enough to be appealing. Even a little.

She rocked back in her seat—and looked up to see Ronan in the doorway. His tie was askew, his hair rumpled. There was blood on his knuckles.

Absently Ronan cradled his hand. Who'd have thought Charlie Wakefield had such a hard jaw?

He relived his satisfaction at the memory of Wakefield's stunned face as he'd crashed to the ground. It had been small enough revenge for the devastation the bastard had inflicted on Cleo and on Marina, but it was a start.

Wakefield didn't look nearly so cocky now that his net value had plummeted by over fifty percent. Even with the help of his family contacts it would take him years of hard work to rebuild what he'd lost.

Now, *that* was satisfying.

Ronan smiled to himself as he walked into the sitting room, but pulled up short, horrified at what he saw.

Marina was there. Huddled in a corner of the sofa. She had her arms wrapped round herself and she was as pale as a wraith. He strode across the room. If Wakefield had hurt her…

He slammed to a stop within a few paces. Close enough to discern her flooded eyes, tear-streaked cheeks and full, trembling lower lip.

And the way she flinched as he reached out to her.

Something closed like a vice round his heart.

Scared—of him? The realisation was a punch to the gut, paralysing him where he stood.

'Marina.' His voice was hoarse. 'Don't look at me like that.'

She blinked and wiped her eyes with the back of her hand. The childish gesture made something twist inside him. He'd wanted to protect her, but somehow he'd failed her.

Why did she shrink from his outstretched hand?

'Whatever he said, don't believe it. Wakefield's a born liar. You know that.' She must understand that by now. She *knew* what an unprincipled shark Wakefield was. 'He'd say anything to make trouble between us.'

'Where is he?' she whispered, even her voice fragile.

'Gone.' He took a careful step nearer. 'Don't worry about him. Security's seeing him off the premises. He can't harm you.'

He was damned if he knew why she'd let Wakefield into the house. She'd promised not to see him alone again. If it hadn't been for Mrs Sinclair's urgent call, interrupting his meeting, he might not even have learned about Wakefield's visit. The thought of that creep alone with Marina made his blood boil. It was obvious he'd injured her somehow.

Then he noticed the papers, splayed across her knees and spilling down onto the floor.

'What are those, Marina? What are all the papers?' He kept his voice low and even, as he would with an injured animal that was scared of more pain. She'd had enough drama already with Wakefield, that was clear. His job now was to rectify the damage, even though it meant holding back from her, waiting to hear about it rather than tugging her straight into his arms.

Her dark eyes were huge and anguished in her pale face. 'Copies of commercial papers.' Her voice was colourless, tearing at his conscience. 'The sale of my house.' She paused and cleared her throat. 'The transfer of Marina Enterprises to you.'

Hell! No wonder she looked as pale as a ghost. She was in shock.

He could imagine the poisonous lies Wakefield had poured into her ears. The callous bastard would have been out for revenge this morning. He couldn't get retribution from Ronan, so he'd gone for a soft target—for Marina. How he must have enjoyed himself. He always had been a sadistic swine.

Ronan's fists clenched. He should have thrashed the bastard unconscious when he had the chance.

But now his priority was Marina. He'd never seen her like this. Even that first night, when she'd collapsed with nervous and physical exhaustion after confronting Wakefield. Then she'd been weak, unsteady, but filled with fighting determination. She'd stood up for herself with a courage that had grabbed at his heart.

But the fight had seeped out of her now. She looked defeated. Dejected. He couldn't stand it.

He reached out and took her hands in his. She tried to resist, to push him away as he sat on the sofa beside her, but he was having none of that. He faced her, knees pressed against her thigh, holding her clenched fists, ice-cold in his hands.

She scared the hell out of him.

'Tell me,' he demanded.

'He said you only ever wanted the company for yourself.' Her voice shook. 'That you tricked me…'

Ronan stared into her blind eyes, desperately searching for his vibrant, passionate Marina. This wasn't her. She was so passive.

'I don't want Marina Enterprises,' he said urgently. 'Let's get that straight right now. I've never sought to take it over, and I haven't schemed to get it for myself.'

Something flickered in her eyes. 'But Wakefield signed it over to you.'

'That was just another tactic of his.' Ronan squeezed her

hands, worried by their coldness. He should get her something for shock, but he couldn't leave her, even for a moment.

'Wakefield was lying.' Her eyes still had that awful blank look of pain and he hurried to explain. 'He must have planned this from the moment he realised he'd have to relinquish the company. By the time my legal people told me he was making the transfer to me, rather than you and your brother, I decided to go with it. Better to have the company safely away from him first. Then we could settle the rest later. That's what I've been doing today—organising a transfer to the Lucchesi family.'

She blinked, and he felt a tremor run through her.

'It's true,' he urged, desperate for her to believe him. 'Your brother Sebastian is at the meeting right now. You can call him.'

She shook her head. 'You didn't tell me,' she whispered.

'No.' His conscience smote him. If he'd been willing to take a risk, to trust Marina as she deserved, none of this would have happened.

His gaze dropped to her mouth. Her bottom lip was swollen where she'd bitten it. He wanted to lean across and kiss it better, pull her against him and keep her close.

'And you bought my house.' It wasn't a statement. It was an accusation.

He looked down to the papers strewn round her feet. How did he explain? His motives hadn't been at all pure. She'd think him manipulative, and she'd just been burned by a master manipulator. Would she judge him to be as bad as Wakefield? He'd wondered that himself, especially when he'd been unable to harness his libido enough to leave her alone while she came to grips with her grief and pain. Why should she see him as any different? That was the dread that woke him in a cold, terrified sweat far too often.

But he had to take that risk.

He took a deep breath and pulled her close, telling himself she needed the body warmth to counteract her shock. The pathetic truth was that he was desperate to have her safe in his arms. She held herself stiffly in his embrace, but she was there, warm and soft, where she belonged.

'Yes, I bought the house. You needed money fast. So I bought it. And I requested a quick settlement.'

She pulled back enough to see his face, and speared him with a look that demanded the truth. He was relieved to see there was a little more colour in her cheeks.

'Why?'

'I did it because I wanted you.' His voice was harsh. 'It's as simple as that.' He heard his own breathing, laboured and heavy in the throbbing silence. Felt the crash of his heart against his ribcage.

'By the time I'd taken you home from Wakefield's reception, by the time I'd put you to bed and walked out the door, I'd decided you were going to be mine.'

Marina gaped at him and he plunged on. He had nothing to lose now. 'That's why I insisted you play the part of my mistress. Because I wanted you close. I wanted you with *me.* But when I had you here in my home, in my bed, things changed. I realised I needed more.' His heart beat so loud now it was like a jackhammer, thudding through his body. 'I wanted…'

'You wanted?'

'To make you fall for me,' he admitted.

Silence. His pulse reverberated like thunder in his ears as he waited for her response. A haze of sweat dampened his skin as he felt real, gut-wrenching fear.

'I don't understand. Why would you want that? Was it because I was some sort of…novelty?' She didn't meet his eyes but looked down at his collar. He had to lean close to catch her words. 'Was it for a bit of fun, because I was different?'

'Novelty! Is that what he said? When I get my hands on that gutter trash I'll—'

'Forget Wakefield and answer my question.' Her whisper brought him up short.

'Oh, honey. You didn't believe that, did you? You couldn't have! Don't you know you're gorgeous? Don't you know I'd do anything to keep you with me?'

Huge, pain-shadowed eyes met his. 'All I know is that you lied to me.'

She'd stabbed him in the heart. And he deserved it. He knew it even as the pain lanced through him.

'You're right.' He heaved in some oxygen. He couldn't seem to catch his breath. 'I lied to you, Marina.'

'Why? Why would you want to hurt me?'

He laughed then, the sound bitter. He'd been worse that Wakefield. At least she'd known what to expect from him.

'I didn't want to hurt you, Marina. Believe me. I—' He swallowed hard and forced himself to continue. 'I wanted you to fall in love with me. Like I'd fallen for you.'

Silence throbbed between them, alive with the sound of his breathing, harsh and rapid. Expectant.

Her eyes looked huge, as if with shock.

Would she, could she, forgive him?

'Well, you managed that,' she murmured at last.

'What?' He'd seen her lips move, but… Had she really said it? 'What did you say?'

Her eyes held his, and in that single, glorious moment he knew. The weight of the last weeks, the horror of unaccustomed uncertainty, lifted from his shoulders, making him dizzy from relief. And around his chest the searing band of pain vanished as he took his first clear breath since he'd seen Wakefield, trying to escape out through the front gate.

'You heard me,' she said. Her lips curved in a tiny smile, and her eyes fell from his as if she were suddenly shy.

In one surge of movement he clasped her to him, close enough to imprint their bodies together. Nothing had ever felt so good. Not even their frantic, passionate lovemaking. For what could compare with knowing his love was reciprocated? And by such a woman. *His* magnificent, sultry, sexy, soon-to-be wife.

'I love you, Marina.' He paused and listened to the satisfying sound of it echo in the air. 'It's taken me long enough to admit it. I kept pretending to myself it was simply lust I felt. And the need to keep you safe. But I was wrong.'

He let his hands slide down over her, slowly caressing. 'And I was a coward. I didn't want to tell you until I was sure you needed me too.'

He leaned close and pressed a kiss on her jaw. Another on the tender spot just below her ear. She tasted like paradise. He circled her ear with his tongue and felt her shiver in his embrace.

He'd never get enough of her. Never.

'You scared the living daylights out of me when you talked about moving out.'

'I was trying to be independent,' she said in a muffled voice. 'You never told me how you felt.'

'That's because I was a damned idiot.' He smiled against her hair, inhaling her fresh, sexy scent. He revelled in the feel of her against him, returning his embrace, her hands stroking restlessly.

'Tell me,' he urged, determined to overcome that one last vestige of fear.

'You're so bossy.'

'Tell me,' he urged, lifting her face to his, 'or I won't kiss you.'

She was smiling now, with her whole face, a wide, wondrous grin that made his heart stutter.

'I love you. I thought that was pathetically obvious.' And then her lips were on his, demanding, persuading, clinging.

He fell into her as if she was his haven. She welcomed him as if she'd never let him go. Her lips were so soft, her mouth so deliciously seductive under his. Her luscious body pressed up against his, driving him inevitably out of his mind. Kissing Marina always short-circuited his brain.

His woman. Warm and wonderful and oh-so-right in his arms. His world began and ended with her.

'I knew from the first that you were mine,' he gasped minutes later, as he fought for breath. He didn't bother to mask the satisfaction in his tone, or the possessiveness of his touch as he sculpted her body with his hands.

'But I looked—'

'Gorgeous,' he whispered against her ear. 'Even in that god-awful suit. Full of fire and passion. Standing up against that bully Wakefield as if you could take on the whole world to protect your family. It was no wonder I fell in love with you.'

'Really?' Even now there was doubt in her voice.

'Marina Lucchesi, you are one stunningly gorgeous woman.' He watched her eyes widen at the words. He hoped that this time she'd believe him. 'You're clever and capable and sexy as hell.'

'Yet I practically had to beg you to make love to me the first time.' She looked away, but he caught her chin and tilted her face so she couldn't avoid him.

'I was trying to do the honourable thing. I wanted you so badly it was killing me. But I knew you were hurting. You'd lost your father, your home, your whole future. You were injured and unsure of yourself. I had no right to force you into intimacy. You were a virgin, for God's sake!'

She shook her head. 'You didn't force me into anything, Ronan. It was my choice, my own free will.'

'And you'll stay? Of your own free will?' He had to hear her say it.

She nodded, a gentle smile curving her lips. 'I'll stay.'

'You're the only woman for me, Marina.' Her dark eyes held him spellbound as his pledge echoed between them.

'So you're after a long-term lover?' Her eyebrow arched inquisitively after a moment.

'Hell, no.' He pulled her tight against him. 'My mother and Cleo are flying over from Perth this weekend, to welcome you into the family. They're all agog to meet you. But I made them wait till I was sure of you.'

'Ah, so Marina Enterprises was going to be a bribe? To persuade me to marry you?'

His heart thudded again as he saw her sweet, teasing smile. He shook his head. 'No, that's already been signed, sealed and delivered. I admit I thought it would help my cause when I handed the documents over to you today as a surprise, at a nice, *intimate* lunch. But I was relying on my natural charm to convince you.'

He lowered his head to take her mouth again, but instead felt the press of her fingers against his lips.

'You've forgotten something,' she said. 'If you want a wife you need to ask me first. That's the traditional way.' There was a glint of laughter in her dark eyes. 'Maybe I'll need persuading.'

Immediately he bent and swept her up into his arms. He pulled her close against his heart, where she belonged. Then he turned and strode to the stairs.

'I'm counting on it,' he said with a grin.

If you love strong, commanding men—
you'll love this miniseries...

Men who can't be tamed...or so they think!

THE SICILIAN'S MARRIAGE ARRANGEMENT

by Lucy Monroe

Hope is overjoyed when sexy Sicilian tycoon Luciano proposes marriage. Hope is completely in love with her gorgeous husband—until Luciano confesses he had had no choice but to wed her....

On sale in February...buy yours today!

Brought to you by your favorite Harlequin Presents authors!

Coming in March:

WANTED: MISTRESS AND MOTHER
by Carol Marinelli,
Book #2616

www.eHarlequin.com HPRUTH0207

HARLEQUIN®
Presents®